MW01108227

Intimate *Chaos*

Liza,
Thank-you for your
support. I hope you
enjoy!

6/7/08

Happy Pride

Intimate *Chaos*

Cheril N. Clarke

Dodi Press – New York, NY

What others are saying:

"*Intimate Chaos* has set the standard in the way a story dealing with alternative relationships or any relationship for that matter should be written. The story takes you deep inside the lives of two women dealing with everyday problems we all face in relationships. If you love intrigue, drama, hot steamy sex, spirituality, strong characters, and did I say DRAMA you will love *Intimate Chaos*." —Lesley Hal, Author of "Blind Temptations"

"Clarke can write...*Intimate Chaos* is an interesting read, with lots of lesbian drama and a story line that keeps you engaged. A great summer read!" —Kathy Belge, Lesbian Life Columnist, About.com

"*Intimate Chaos* is a heart wrenching story about love lost and found. Clarke tells the story in first person...I felt Sadira's happiness, joy and pain. There were also times when I wanted to shake the hell out of Sadira and wondered if someone could really be that love struck. Then I laughed and reflected. Yep, they can because I've been there before."—Esther "Ess" Mays, www.looseleaves.org

Intimate Chaos

This book is a work of fiction, but it was inspired by actual events. Resemblance to persons, locations, or characters real or fictional, living or deceased is entirely coincidental and unintentional except where the author has written permission for such characterization.

Copyright ©2004 Dodi Press
Original copyright under the title "What Do I Know about Love?" ©2003
This book was published by Dodi Press, and printed in the United States of America in 2005.

No part of this publication may be reproduced or transmitted in any form or by any means, electronic, mechanical, or digital, including photocopying, recording, or otherwise, or by any information storage and retrieval system without the prior written permission of the copyright holder. Requests for such permission should be addressed to: Dodi Press, 244 Fifth Av., 2nd Fl., Suite J260, New York, NY 10001.

ISBN: 0-9767273-0-7

Rev.8/22/05

Acknowledgements

This book would not be what it is without the help of many people. I would like to extend a warm thank you to the following individuals and organizations for all of your love and support of this project.

I would like to thank my partner and friend, Monica R. Bey. The revision process would have been impossible without you pushing me to change it from a good book to a *great* book. Thank you for your support, even when it put you in very awkward positions. I love, and truly value you. Thanks for standing by me no matter what. I am forever indebted to you.

Sandra K. Poole, Jeremy Braggs, Derrick Cotton, Yolanda Hill, Kelli Costley, Ebony Farashuu, Gena L. Garrison, Richard Parks Jr., Kandyss Watson, Neahle Jones, J.J. Johnson and the rest of *Soul City*, I appreciate you. Susan Webley, Cheryl McPherson, Lynne Womble, Paris and Eshey Harris and the entire *SABLE Magazine* team, thank you.

SPAN and the self-publishing list, thanks for helping me learn the *business* of writing. Lori Bryant-Woolridge, Shel Horowitz, Keiba Young, Fernando Rodriguez, Byron James, Dr. Michelle Hutchinson and Chandra S. Taylor, thank you for your support. My family, I thank you for your support. My editorial consultant, Charles Patterson, thanks for helping me make the final touches on this book. Thanks to N'Digo Design for the wonderful website and cover design!

Aja, Excelsior, Deli, Mo' Love, Siyah, s.e.a, Eons, DJ K-Starr, DJ ChocolateGirlWonder, and DJ One, I want to thank you ladies and the entire *vim* artist family of 2003. *vim* allowed me to nurture my stage presence and build a following around New York City. Thank you for the exposure. Donna "Dee" Shands, I especially want to thank you for giving me my own space in your MSN Group. It was there that this story was born. To the ladies of LS, thanks for nagging me, the first draft of this book was completed in three months because of you.

In Loving Memory of:
…Turhan Bey…
and
…Vivienne Tucker…

This book was inspired by and is dedicated to:

...Juliette...

Part I

Chapter 1

Dear Sadira,

    I feel like I need to come clean. My heart and mind are telling me to strip myself of all suppressed feelings. The truth is I don't want you to leave. No one has been able to penetrate my soul like you. Since we've known each other, I've had revelation after revelation. Forget the nonsense of me holding on to my pride; I need you.

    I can't change the course of this lifetime, nor can I go back and make right what I know I did wrong in the past. Moreover, I'm not asking you to make me a priority over someone you love or even give me a second chance because honestly I don't deserve one. I just want to continue to experience and to love you in any way that you will allow me to. I just need you as my friend. That is all.

    I've had experiences with you that transcend any night or moment of passion. You made love to my mind and climaxed inside my soul. I feel like there are tiny pieces of you all over and inside of me. Maybe that's why it's so difficult to let you go. You are in me, and I can still feel you.

    *I will always wonder what could have been if I had only done it all differently. And I'll always have love for you. All I ask is that you stay close to me, at least as a friend, until our next lifetime where we can perhaps **just be.***

    Until we see each other again, let us continue to look at ourselves.

Love always,

Jessie

Jessie's last words played over and over as I reflected on our relationship before falling asleep. After all we'd been through, we seemed to be back to square one. In the morning, a loud chatter of voices streamed through my clock radio, waking me up. After yawning and blankly looking around my new apartment, I sat back and thought about the turns my life had taken. From New York to Miami to Atlanta, and then back to New York again, I'd been up, down, and around, all in search of love and happiness. But I wanted to get out, to disentangle myself from the exhausting search entirely. The chaos started three years ago when I met Jessie. I was 25 years old at the time.

It was a cool Friday morning in August when I stepped outside. I walked three blocks up to the 116th Street subway station observing my neighborhood that was simultaneously comical and sad, as if both were needed for it to function properly. I lived in a basement apartment of a brownstone in Harlem, New York, and everyone had an "I'm going to get mine" mentality. *Mine* could mean anything from getting their kids into college to selling $500 worth of Newport cigarettes on the street or vending incense sticks in front of The Disney Store on 125th Street. I lived in a hub of hustlers.

At the subway entrance, I descended into the lower level of the city where life was just as fluid as above ground. A man was playing steel drums, and farther down the subway platform, a homeless person was shouting biblical verses at the top of his lungs. He pleaded for everyone to accept God before it was too late. "We're in the end times!" he yelled as the B train pulled into the station. I secured my bag on my shoulder and stepped aboard. I worked the morning shift as an audio engineer at WSOL, a radio station in midtown.

The day went by quickly, and I left early to pick up my twin sister, Khedara, from La Guardia Airport. Her flight had been delayed twice.

"My flight's definitely leaving soon, so make sure you're there because I'm exhausted."

"Yeah, yeah, I'll be there," I told her. "I'm getting on a train right now. I'll call you back."

"All right, bye."

During the ride, my eyes met a beautiful woman nodding off to sleep diagonally across from me. She had a slim build and a small pendant hanging from a necklace that dipped into her cleavage. Usually I wasn't good at picking up women, but she was so striking I felt I had to say something to her. I told myself that if she were single, I would do whatever it took to make her mine. Looking at her, I saw my future, period.

Her flawless complexion reminded me of a honey graham just waiting to be devoured. I tried to be inconspicuous as I watched her rouse herself and remove her jacket, hoping that her blue-gray eyes would not meet mine as I took in everything from her black high-heels to her neat dreadlocks pulled back just enough to reveal her smooth shoulders. *Damn,* I thought as my eyes passed over her well-toned arms. I tried to be discreet, but I could not keep myself from staring at her bosom classily encased in a tan corset top. Her leather pants hugged her in places I had no business thinking about, and when I noticed the rainbow bracelet on her wrist, I prayed it wasn't just a fashion statement, because in my mind rainbow bracelet meant gay or at least bisexual. She closed her eyes again.

I wanted to strike up a conversation badly, but I didn't know what to say. Luckily I had a flyer for a gay event on me, so I decided to use it as a conversation starter. I waited for her to open her eyes so I could make contact, but she only adjusted herself in her seat without opening them. A few moments later she opened them and locked them on mine. I froze. She smiled at me before closing her eyes again. I appreciated the smile and hoped it was an invitation to approach her. I nervously tried to get my pick-up line together in my head. *I'm no good at this. What if she rejects me?* Seconds later she opened her eyes and began looking around to see if her stop was coming up. *Oh, just say something, quickly.* Finally I found the courage to get up and sit next to this beautiful woman.

"Excuse me?" I said.

"Yes?"

"Um, I just wanted to give you this flyer." As she read it I added, "By the way, I like your bracelet." *That was corny,* I thought to myself as I got up to return to my seat.

"Thank you," she replied and smiled. She read over the flyer some more before looking up at me. She stared at me and then smiled again. I smiled back and nodded for her to come over, and she did.

"I feel like I know you from somewhere," she began.

"I don't know, maybe. What's your name?"

"Jessie." She extended her hand.

As I shook her hand, I noticed how soft and well manicured it was. "Hmm, well, it's nice to meet you. My name is Sadira, and maybe I just have 'one of those faces'." We exchanged glances.

There was an uncomfortable silence for a moment as the train approached my stop. "Um, I have to get off here, but I'd like to stay in contact with you. May I have your e-mail address?" She looked surprised, probably because I asked for her e-mail address instead of her phone number, but she gave it to me anyway.

"Yeah, sure," she said, reaching in her purse and handing me her business card. "My contact info is all there." After I got off the train and it continued on its way, I watched the small view of Jessie in the window disappear.

I arrived on time to pick up Khedara. She looked different. Her hair was longer than the identical cut we both used to wear, and she'd gained a little weight. We greeted each other and chatted a bit. I told her about Jessie. Later we went to Times Square and hung out. We had an early dinner at Applebee's before going to the famed Nuyorican Poets Café on the lower east side of Manhattan.

Chapter 2

It was Monday afternoon, and Khedara had gone back to Atlanta. I'd e-mailed Jessie a "nice to meet you" greeting with my phone number, but she hadn't responded yet. Though I had a busy week ahead of me, I hoped to make time to see her if she were available. *If I only had the chance, I know I can make her mine.*

After the rest of my workday dragged by, I went home to take a nap before going to my second job bartending at a nightclub called, Elsie's. It rained that night, and business at the club was slow. By the time I left and got off the bus the rain was crashing down hard. The one block walk to my house left me drenched and freezing. After showering and eating I turned on my computer to check my e-mail, but it was full of newsletters and SPAM, nothing from Jessie. Disappointed, I shut the computer back down and climbed into bed.

The rest of my week flew by. It wasn't until that Friday that I finally received a message from her. It was short, just telling me that she would call soon. I waited eagerly, but she didn't call, and I had to leave town for the weekend. I wouldn't be back until Sunday.

My return flight was delayed so I decided to check my e-mail at the airport hoping Jessie had sent me something, anything. I nearly jumped out of my skin when I saw that there was a message from her. *Just writing to write* was the subject.

Hello Sadira,

I hope you are well today. Hmm. Where do I begin? I have a feeling that you've been waiting to know more about me. Well, I live alone in Queens. My family is from the Dominican Republic though I did not grow up there. I grew up in the Bronx, and my family still lives there. I'm twenty-six. That's all I can think of for right now. I'm kind of tired but have been meaning to e-mail you. It's just that I've been so busy lately with work. I'm an IT consultant for a law firm in Midtown. Plus I regularly draw comics for a small newspaper on the side to keep my creative side fulfilled. Art is my first love but my mother saw to it that I finished school and obtained a career rather than just a job. Well, I did and I feel like I'm constantly on the go. You'd think I would have learned my lesson about working so much since it cost me a previous relationship, but I haven't learned a thing. I have my eyes set on building a strong career, and I figure the person for me will be able to handle my schedule.

You know it's funny that as soon as I typed that I got a feeling of dishonesty, like I'm just lying to protect myself. Maybe I work excessively to avoid letting any one person get to close to me. I can't get hurt that way. Well, I've said way more than I planned to so I'll end it here. I'll be in touch.

Until we see each other again, let us continue to look at ourselves,
Jessie

I thought about her signature first. It was interesting to say the least. Bits and pieces of her e-mail stood out. Her words skimmed the surface of her previous relationship without saying how and when it actually ended. She was afraid of getting hurt, that was very clear. I wondered how I could move things along with her without seeming too eager. I was sure I wouldn't hurt her. I sat in silence and decided against responding immediately. I needed to think over and absorb her words. Though I initially asked her for her e-mail address as opposed to her phone number, I had no idea that the majority of our "getting to know each other" conversations would take place on-line. We sent pictures back and forth and talked about various things from music to things in the news. She never returned e-mails or phone calls in a timely manner though.

There were some nights that we would be on instant messenger for hours before finally talking on the phone until the sun came up. I was trying to find out more about how she felt about me, but she wouldn't stay on the subject long. "I do like you, Sadira. I just want to take it slow," she said. That was enough for me to want to stay around. In the meantime, I made mental notes of all the things she said in our conversations that gave me clues to what she may have also been feeling.

I took advantage of the fact that the Internet turned out to be our main line of communication. One day I decided to surprise her with a full-blown power point presentation. *That will get her attention*, I thought and it did. It included songs she might enjoy, photos that she'd sent me pasted next to mine, clip art of things that reflected what she liked. I wrote: *Let me demolish the pain left behind by others into pieces that are so small that they rebel against the power of memory to recall their existence. I don't want to be with you just because you're pretty or just to say 'I got that,' to my friends. Sex is the last thing on my mind and if it would make you comfortable, I would wait up to a year before being intimate with you. I don't care.* The next day came the breakthrough. She answered: *Okay, you know you have me grinning from ear to ear. That was so sweet! Sadira, you definitely caught my attention. Today you've made me smile bigger and brighter than I have in a very long time. (Right now I'm trying to show you the pearly whites through the screen). I like the fact that you can make me laugh, smile, and feel special. This feeling right now is intoxicating. That is a weird word for describing how I'm feeling right now but it feels good and that's how I can best describe it. So far you've pursued me differently than any other woman. I appreciate your individuality and your own sense of style in doing things. You hardly know me but these types of actions are what really move me. They really allow me to appreciate and admire the soul of a person. THANK YOU SO MUCH. I don't know how many times I can say how much I appreciate this...let me try:*

THANK YOU, THANK YOU, THANK YOU, THANK YOU, THANK YOU, THANK YOUUUUUUUUU!!!!!!!!!!!!!!!

All right, I'm done. But really thanks, you're a sweetheart.
Until we see each other again, let's continue to look at ourselves,
Jessie

Jessie made me work for her attention, but when I finally got it, the feeling I had inside of me was hard to describe. Whether I got a glowing response or only got a brief e-mail or talked to her for five minutes, for some reason she always made my day by just existing in it. There was an unexplainable connection between Jessie and me from the first day we met. However strange it may have been, it was real and getting stronger.

There were days that we both took off work just to spend time with each other. We talked about our personal goals in life and how we planned on achieving them. We held hands, hugged and built moments never to be forgotten. It felt good to have her full attention.

"There is something rare about you," she said one day. We were sitting on the steps of the Metropolitan Museum of Art.

"And what might that be, Jessie?"

"I don't know. It's just the way you make me feel inside."

"Hmm," I said, leaning back and absorbing her words.

She inched closer to me. "You make me feel confused on the inside."

"I don't understand," I said, putting my arm around her.

"Oh boy, I cannot believe I am even telling you this, but you make me feel weak because I can't control my feelings. Yet at the same time you make me feel as if I have the power and strength of ten gods. I am stuck in between a state of confusion and euphoria if that makes any sense."

"Wow," I said, then smiled. I was happy that Jessie seemed to feel the same way I did about her. *If she'd just give us a fair chance, we might just fall in love.* It was a good feeling.

She became silent herself and stared at the buses, taxis, and tourists bustling by on Manhattan's busy Fifth Avenue. We'd spent a good three hours at the museum. Later we went out for dinner and then to see a play before retiring for an evening at home alone at her place in Queens. Her love for contemporary art was very evident in her apartment. There were framed prints hanging on the walls and sculptures in corners. A warm blue and cream color scheme surrounded a glass table with a peculiar design carved into the center of it in the living room.

Jessie's bedroom was a bit darker than the rest of her place. Sandy brown sheets and a thick black comforter covered her bed.

"That's nice," I said admiring an abstract painting above her bed.

"Thank you. I did that when I was in college. It's one of my favorites."

"Wow, that's an original of yours?"

"Yes."

"Nice," I repeated and she smiled.

We went back in her living room, talked and watched TV for a while, but she started to get sleepy. After taking separate showers we went in Jessie's bedroom to lie down. I kissed her on the cheek and lay still for a moment. I wasn't sure if I should try to go further or just hold her and go to sleep. I knew what *I* wanted to do, but she'd told me more than once that she wanted to take things slow. As we lay in the dark I couldn't help but kiss her on the back of the neck. She tensed up a little bit. "Relax," I whispered. I slowly ran my right hand down the side of her body while kissing her neck. She turned to face me, and I leaned in to kiss her on the lips. We continued for a moment before the phone rang and pulled us out of the moment.

"Let it ring," I said.

"No, I should get it." She appeared relieved that something broke the moment.

Frustrated, I lay there listening to her one sided conversation.

"My mother," she said after hanging up. "She wants me to see her tomorrow."

"Oh."

Climbing back into bed she said, "Sadira, maybe we should wait a little longer, you know. I just want to…"

"Take things slow, I know." I didn't want what I said to come out in annoyance, but wasn't sure if it did. "If that's what you want, then okay."

She snuggled up close to me, putting her head on my chest, and I put my arm around her. I kissed her forehead and tried to go to sleep, but I was having a difficult time. I pulled her on top of me and moved my body upward into hers. She began to follow suit but stopped. "I'm sorry," I said. "Sorry."

She looked at me curiously then got off and back into my arms. Eventually, we drifted off into sleep.

Over the next two weeks everything felt just right. We went to dinners, movies, karaoke bars and clubs. Our e-mails still flowed back and forth as if we were separated by distance. There was something about conversing seriously in that manner that just made things easier to say for the both of us, I think. Some days we would chat on an instant messenger for hours rather than talk on the phone. *Strange*, I thought, but it felt normal for us.

Time went by rather quickly and it seemed to rain almost every day. As September crept into October, I spoke with Jessie even more and saw her a couple of times. Those two times weren't dates though. She just came by the club where I worked, said a few words to me and that didn't count because there was always a ton of people there. It was far from personal. Then the phone calls slowed down again although we continued to communicate through instant messenger and e-mail. I kept a folder with all of our e-mails, and at first I thought something was wrong with me. *Why the hell am I keeping all of our e-mails?* But for some reason I kept them, and I'd never done that before. She had a hell of a hold on me.

Jessie and I had a real back and forth, or maybe "yo-yo" is a better word to describe it. No matter what though, with every passing day my intrigue, care, and feelings for her grew. In the meantime, her feelings for me also peeked out from behind her shield of fear. Jessie had a wall built around her heart to protect it from being broken, but I was determined to penetrate it, even if it meant removing one brick at a time.

Over the next couple of weeks we saw each other a few times and spoke on the phone about every other day. Our evening schedules conflicted because of my job at the club, but I felt that she could have made more of an effort to see me at least for lunch during the day. We both worked in Manhattan one subway stop away from each other, but whenever Jessie agreed to a lunch date she would cancel an hour before saying she had to deal with clients or be in a meeting or something. It pissed me off. It hurt my feelings. It confused me. But no matter how many times she pulled her disappearing act, I always welcomed her back.

I prayed about it, asking for guidance. The tentacles of her flawed personality wrapped themselves around me tightly. I felt my feelings of both anger and attraction getting out of control. The angrier I got with Jessie for standing me up strangely made getting back with her seem all the sweeter. I missed her terribly when I was out of touch with her.

Although I e-mailed her enough love letters and poems to litter the world, I couldn't figure her out. Why was she still so withdrawn? She would respond to my acts of kindness with appreciation but then suddenly disappear without warning. Jessie was definitely sending me mixed signals.

I remember one night when I was totally fed up, lying alone thinking of her and wanting to call with my head aching. Instead of calling, I just let my body drift off into a restless sleep only to be awakened by a call from her at three o'clock in the morning as if it were twelve noon.

I picked up the receiver. "Hello?"

"Hey, Sadira!"

"Damn, Jessie, it's the middle of the night."

"I'm sorry. I'll let you go back to sleep then."

"No, wait, it's okay. I just wish you would show a little consideration about what time it is."

"Sadira," she said with a sigh, "I just called because I miss you. I can't help what time it is. I thought you'd be happy to hear from me."

"I am, Jessie. I'm sorry for snapping at you." Turning and lying on my back, I smiled. I was glad she called. *The things I put up with,* I thought. My usual tolerance for games and foolishness with women had reached a new level with Jessie. She told me about her day and that she'd just got in from a club with her friend, Janae.

"A party?" I felt aggravated. "You don't have five minutes for me, but you can go to a fucking club?"

"What?" she asked as if she didn't see anything wrong. "We just went out for a dance, it's not like I went out on a date with someone."

"Jessie, what do you mean 'what'? This is bullshit."

"Fine," she said with a pout. "Next time I won't call you. The next time you cross my mind I'll push you out and forget about you."

"No wait, it's okay." *What is wrong with you?* I heard my mind ask. *Let that bitch **go**.* "Jessie," I said, taking a deep breath, "I'll call you tomorrow, okay?"

"All right," she said and hung up.

You're a damn fool, I thought to myself as I tried to go back to sleep. I had to get up early for my day job at the radio station.

I was upset. I had willingly walked into her world without taking into account what might happen to my heart relying on her. I made the mistake of thinking she would change, but as soon as I thought she was getting better, she put an abrupt halt to our interactions. We would go to the movies one day, and then I wouldn't hear from her again. No phone calls or notes, no goodbye, absolutely nothing. I didn't understand Jessie. In my frustration, I decided to call my sister.

"Hey, Khedara," I said.

"What's up, girl?"

"Not much. Hey, do you remember that girl I met on the train when you were up here?"

"Yeah, you said she had locks or something, right?"

"Yes, her."

"So, what about her? Are you in love with her?"

"No!" I insisted, secretly questioning my answer. "But we did start talking and I'm intrigued by her."

"But?"

I sighed. "But... she just keeps popping in and out of my life. Now I see her, now I don't."

"So speak up or cut her off." Even as Khedara said it, I already knew what I had to do. It wasn't really a matter of cutting Jessie off because she left me. It was a matter of not welcoming her back after her exits. I was annoyed and frustrated, but I didn't want to give up hope. *She just needs some time*, I thought.

"Hey, Sadira, I hate to cut this short, but I have to take care of something. You know what you have to do. Call me back and don't be a punk about speaking up."

"I'm not a punk," I said, remembering the last time Jessie turned me into mush.

"Whatever." Khedara always called me a punk or soft when it came to relationships. "Bye," she said.

"Talk to you later."

Although I knew Khedara was right, I was reluctant to say anything to Jessie. I didn't call or try to e-mail her. As a matter of fact, I took her off of my buddy list so that I wouldn't be able to see when she was online and wouldn't be tempted to send her a message. I decided to just let her be wherever she was. Deep down though, I hoped she'd find her way back to me on her own.

I'd just started adjusting to being alone again as December came and snow gift-wrapped the city like an early Christmas present. Green and white decorations were along the traffic lights on 125th Street as people hustled more than usual to make extra money. They were selling hats, scarves, incense, and one man was even selling colored contacts, lotion, and lighters all on the same table. I walked my normal route to the train station with my baseball cap pulled down low. I didn't want to be bothered or have to make eye contact with anyone. Christmas did nothing but remind me of how lonely I felt and how much I missed Jessie, but I was too proud to call her.

My birthday came without anything out of the ordinary happening. I only worked a half day at the radio station and left the club early too. I went about my business, treating myself to a few extra things. At about 10:20 that night, my cell phone beeped to let me know I had a voice mail message. I'd just come out of the subway by my house and missed the call, so I immediately checked my voice mail. Though I had waited all day to hear from Jessie, the actual sound of her voice saddened me. I didn't know if I should have been grateful that she remembered my birthday, or angry that she had the nerve to call so late. *Whatever,* I thought, and tried to brush off my thoughts of Jessie. She knew all day that it was my birthday, and all she could do was leave me a 12-second message saying happy birthday? It hurt more than I wanted to acknowledge.

The next morning when I went in to work, I bumped into the morning show host, Devonte. He was the station's very own ghetto talk show host. He kept the ratings up and the phones ringing. I couldn't stand him at first, but he grew on me. I'm not sure if his growth was in a way like a brother or like a fungus, but I liked him. In fact, I often found myself telling him personal things.

"What's wrong with you?" he asked.

"I'm fine," I insisted.

"Women problems?"

"Yep."

"Didn't I tell you to leave that knotty-headed girl alone, Sadira?"

I had told him about my problem with Jessie, but didn't respond to his question.

"How many times are you two going to break up and get back together? Sadira, you break up for a *reason.* That's all I'm going to say on that."

"I know, I know."

"You know you're my nigga, right?"

I looked at him and sighed. "Yes."

"Okay then, I'm just trying to look out for you, shorty. I have to go. I'll catch up with you later. Put a smile on your face, girl." He turned and walked off.

The day went by quickly as usual. My train ride was hot and crowded, and the normal 20-minute commute turned into an hour. Being trapped in front of a man whose breath was bad enough to smell from behind, the sight of an oncoming panhandler, and the sound of kids walking through the car hawking M & M candies was enough to prompt me to turn up the volume on my CD player and lose myself in the lyrics of Tupac.

As soon as I emerged from the subway, my cell phone rang. It was Khedara.

"What's up, sis?"

"I feel so annoyed," she said with a sigh.

"What's wrong with you?"

"First of all, this is my sixth day of working twelve-hour shifts. My head is pounding, and my supervisor set down a deadline that can't possibly be met."

"But you have an assistant, right?"

"She's called in sick three days in a row, and I dare her to come back in here without a doctor's note. I've been waiting for a reason to fire her anyway."

"Damn, what did she do?"

"Second of all," she continued, disregarding my question. "Not only do I have a zillion numbers to crunch, we have this new guy in technical support, Franz, from some country or another and he smells dead! Ever since he installed my new computer, he keeps stopping by to see if everything works fine. Don't you think if it didn't work, I would call him?"

"Yes but…"

"Hold on, Sadira," she said, cutting me off. I'd already walked to my house and was sitting on the steps. "Yes," she continued, "so he thinks he's sexy or suave or debonair or something and it makes him want to flirt with me. Now you know he picked the *wrong* one to flirt with, right? He just put some Christmas cookies on my desk and now he keeps looking to see if I'm going to eat them. Girl, I'm hungrier than a runaway slave, but every time I look at the cookies I smell funk!"

"Khedara, slow down."

"And that's probably because he came in my damn office and had the nerve to plant his sour debonair ass on the corner of my desk when he left the cookies. He left a fucking stench. I'm about to snap!"

"Calm down, calm down." I was trying so hard not to laugh that I literally had tears streaming down my face. "Hold on," I told her. I had another call. It was Jessie, but she hung up before I could click over. I sighed and went back to Khedara.

"It's time to take my ass home for the day," she said, "or someone is going to get cursed out. Ugh, I feel nauseous. I'm leaving this dreadful place before I vomit. I'll call you later."

"Okay, then."

"Thanks for listening."

"Anytime," I told her and heard her hang up "Sour debonair?" I said out loud to myself and laughed. Damn.

I checked my voicemail hesitantly. *Hey, Sadira it's me Jessie. I was just calling to say hey. I haven't spoken to you in awhile and feel kind of lonely. I'm sorry I haven't called more but I've been going through some things with my family here and have been depressed. I didn't want my mood to rub off on you. I do miss you though. I hope everything is going well. Call me when you can. Bye."*

When I called back, I got her voice mail. There were some things that I wanted to say to her, but I was not sure if I should. I hung up without leaving a message and ended up writing a letter to her instead.

Hey,

Thanks for the birthday wish. I hope that everything you're going through will pass with you getting stronger. You said you feel alone, but you pushed me away, or rather, you ran away. I'll stay away from you if that's what you want. No worries.

I'm not trying to get my feelings too caught up with you or with anyone new right now. Fear has made a home in me. I have to figure out what's wrong with me that people keep abandoning—oh never mind. I assume you have enough to worry about, so I won't add to your emotional strain, but you can call me if you want to. Even if many weeks have passed, my number should still be the same, and, if not, e-mail always works. I said I'd never leave, and I've never gone against what I said I would do. I'm being distant, yet available. Does that make sense? I hope so.

You once said, "Until we see each other again, let's continue to look at ourselves," I will do that and hope you do too.

Sadira Cooper

I wished I could un-send my note after it went off, but it was too late. For the first time I included Jessie in my prayers that night, and tried not to stress over her too much. Time seemed to slow down, and the days felt longer. It was only the second week of December.

Chapter 3

Jessie and I saw each other a couple of days later and picked up like nothing happened. We went to a small Mexican restaurant in the East Village.

"I'm sorry," she said. "I just felt like I was loosing control. I don't like when I can't control my feelings. That's why I pulled away from you."

"So why are you back then, Jessie?" I asked, wiping my mouth with a napkin.

"I missed you. You make me smile."

I sighed. "I don't know how much more of this I can take."

"Sorry."

I was baffled and hadn't a clue what to do. It seemed like no matter what, she'd always be back. I decided to change the subject. "How are things with your family?"

"My mother is great. I'm going up to the Bronx to see her tomorrow. My brother continues to do nothing with himself, and my sisters still don't like me. My father pops in and out, sometimes for weeks at a time. I don't know how my mother puts up with him." Her sentence faded into silence.

I looked at her and sighed, making a mental note about her father's disappearing acts in connection with her own. Then I signaled the waitress for the check before leaving. Despite the cold, we decided to walk along the pier for a while before calling it a night. She faded back into my life just as smoothly as she'd left. And as usual, I opened my arms to receive her.

"Do you miss Miami at all?" she asked, picking up on our conversation in the restaurant.

"No."

"Why not?"

"Jessie, I told you the only feeling I have toward Miami is that it's full of painful memories—memories of being shifted from house to house as an unwanted child."

"So you'd never try to live there again?"

"I seriously doubt it."

"Oh," she said softly and we walked by the water in silence.

My parents died when Khedara and I were six years old. We were away at summer camp when it happened. Trying to recover from a hurricane that caused a power outage for days, our parents made a fatal mistake. They used a fuel generator inside the house and died in their sleep from inhaling pure carbon monoxide.

This tragedy left us in the care of our grandmother, who took care of us for two years but then died of a heart attack. After that we bounced around Miami from one foster home to another until we were eighteen years old. Sometimes we lived all right, but at other times we barely ate one meal a day. At one point we were separated, and I got stuck with a mean old woman, Esther, who had me put in remedial classes and said that I had a learning disorder just so she could get more money for taking care of me, but that was somewhat straightened out when I got to high school. I wanted to be in the band and play the trumpet, but I had to at least have a 2.5 grade point average, so I made friends with "smart kids," who helped me study during after school hours so I could be placed where I rightfully belonged.

Khedara didn't have it as bad. She lived with a progressive family while I was with Esther, who beat me just because she felt like it, but soon my sister and I were together again. That lasted until I left to join the Air Force and Khedara then went off to Spellman College in Atlanta where she stayed after graduating with a degree in accounting.

I knew Jessie wanted to move to Miami. She'd told me that before I told her about my childhood. I'd have to be sure I was spending my life with her to make such a change. The truth was that I also wanted to leave New York, but not for Miami.

"Give me a kiss," Jessie said and I did, but quickly.

The cold was starting to get unbearable, so we walked back to the garage where her cream colored Rav4 was parked. In the back of my mind I wondered why she had asked me about moving to Miami again. It didn't seem as though she was ready to get that serious with me, but I would have been glad if she stopped disappearing and got serious. *Maybe she was finally ready to commit to me,* I thought as we drove to her place.

     We decided to stay in on Christmas Eve. The actual day came and went like any other day. Jessie didn't celebrate it so it was no big deal for either of us. She wouldn't tell me why she didn't celebrate Christmas, but she promised one day she would. I'd called Khedara that morning, but she was volunteering at a soup kitchen.

During the days that followed things started to go smoothly between us. We talked constantly, and she actually followed through on our scheduled dates. Our relationship seemed to be taking a turn for the better. We were actually acting like a couple though there still was no title there and we still hadn't had sex yet. I thought back to when I told her that I'd wait up to a year before having sex if it made her comfortable. *Me and my big mouth.*

"Sadira?"

Her voice pulled me out of my thoughts. "Yeah?"

"Do you want to go out one night this week, maybe Monday or Tuesday?"

"Well, Monday I know I can't but as for Tuesday, sure, why not? Where do you want to go?"

"I was thinking Karma."

"Sounds good." I'd been to Karma quite a few times. It's an open mic lounge where people from all walks of life can express themselves on stage. "I can't stay out really late though because I have to get up at 5 a.m."

"I know you work the first shift for the morning show." Jessie was the type of person who had enough energy to be out all night, go home, shower and go straight to work without sleep when she wanted to. Not me.

"Then okay, we can go. One of these days I'm going to go back on the mic."

"You should. I can tell you have a way with words."

"Yeah, I have notebooks full of stuff, but they're mostly erotic and I'm not sure about sharing them."

She smiled. "Now you know I want to read them, right?"

I blushed. "I'll show you one day. Or I'll just be brave and do it on Tuesday. As a matter of fact, a lot of stuff I wrote is archived on a message board. I'll e-mail you the link if you want to check it out."

"I can't wait to read *and* hear your work." She brushed her thumb against my right cheek before placing a soft kiss on it. At that moment I felt closer to her than I'd ever been allowed to get. She had let her guard down enough to show me that she cared to hear what I had to say. *Finally*.

Monday seemed like a slow day. Jessie and I spoke briefly in the afternoon before I took a nap between jobs. She told me that she went to the message board I'd told her about and read every poem and story I ever posted. That made my day. I was starting to like writing more and more, so there was a lot on the message board. Jessie went back nine months to familiarize herself with the part of me she didn't know existed. The fact that she actually read all of my work really hit home with me. She told me that she felt the best way to get to know a person, especially one in the arts, was through their art.

"Artists reveal a lot more about themselves in their work than they think they do," she said.

She was right and because she'd read my work I decided to go to Queens and pick up the paper that she drew for. Then one day I'd just refer to it out of the blue. I was sure she thought I forgot about it. I fell asleep with a smile on my face.

I woke up from my nap and got dressed for work. It was busy at the club with everyone partying and anticipating the New Year. By the end of the evening I eagerly looked forward to my quiet bus ride home. Shortly after I sat down in a seat on the bus, my cell phone rang

"Hey, you. It's me, Jessie."

"Hi," I said smiling. "What are you doing up?"

"I'm always up."

"Yeah, you are. What's going on?" I shot a smile at the driver, who was looking at me in the mirror. I'd grown accustomed to being on his bus at night and had befriended him. He nodded and kept driving.

"Would you like to see me tonight?" she asked.

"What?"

"I asked if you wanted to see me tonight."

"Yeah, but wait, where are you?"

"I'm driving in Manhattan and I can come by your place if you want."

That caught me off guard. Jessie had never been to my place. It was almost two o'clock in the morning. "Sure," I said. I was exhausted, but there was no way I would say no.

"Okay, how do I get there?" I gave her directions, but since I would actually have to pass where she would go to get to my place, I got off the bus a few stops later and waited for her to pick me up.

"Goodnight," I said to the driver as I stepped off with Jessie still on the phone. Ten minutes later she pulled up, and I got into her Jeep. She had on a black turtleneck and suede pants that clung to her body, and her eyes sparkled under the brim of her hat. They were almost magnetic, sucking me further into her world. Flashing her flawless smile at me, she looked as beautiful as ever. A mysterious sensuality oozed from her very pores.

I got in and leaned to kiss her on the cheek before she put the car back in drive, but as I tried to move back to my seat she pulled me closer and kissed me slow and hard on the lips. Our tongues touched and for the first time we really kissed. I don't know how I managed to be comfortable with moving so slowly with her, but I was. I guess the good thing with waiting to be intimate with Jessie was that with each new touch and graze of our bodies the powers held within them were intense and magnified. Waiting for intimacy with her showed me what it truly felt like to crave another person. After a few minutes of kissing we released each other and got on the West Side Highway en route to my apartment in Harlem.

"Well, this is it," I said as we walked up to my brownstone. "My landlord lives upstairs. He's a little weird but overall okay."

"Okay." She smiled and followed me to my private entrance to the basement. She glimpsed at herself in the mirror that I had next to the door inside. "It smells good in here," She said.

"I leave incense burning during the day." I took her coat and got her something to drink.

"You're place is inviting. It almost seems like it has a glow to it."

She looked around, but didn't say much. It was clean so I wasn't worried about giving her a bad impression. In fact, I was hoping the *glow* she referred to was a good thing. I had tall lamps in the corners that I preferred to use rather than the ceiling light.

"You're a neat freak, aren't you?"

I smiled. "Sort of." My apartment was small, so I really tried to make it look better by not having a lot of furniture and clutter.

"Well, it looks comfortable in here," she said and sat down.

"Good, I want you to be comfortable." We talked for a little while before I convinced her to lay down with me. I put my hand on her stomach and slowly slid it up to her breasts. She didn't stop my advance this time. Instead, she locked her eyes on me. I kissed her while unbuttoning her shirt. She kissed me back and moved closer. I hoped she wasn't going to change her mind because I didn't think I could stop. I wanted her so bad it ached. And fuck, it was the middle of the night, what did she expect?

She stopped kissing me. "Wait."

God damn it. "What? Jessie what's the problem?"

"No. There's no problem. I just want to talk."

"Why? We've been talking. I don't want to talk, I…"

She placed her index finger on my lips and sat up. "Listen."

"No."

"Sadira!"

"Fine."

"I've been thinking." She paused and took a deep breath. "I think we should be exclusive."

"What?"

"I'm saying, Sadira, I want you to be my girl. I want to be the only one you see."

"But weren't you just saying that you wanted to take things slow."

"Shh," she said and came closer to me. She pulled me into her arms and kissed me on the neck.

I was baffled.

"Please?" she said.

I remained silent. I was eager to say yes, but I reminded myself to be cautious with my heart. How could I be sure Jessie wouldn't disappear again? "I don't understand. What made you change your mind?"

"Well, I know I've been in and out with you, but you stayed. Over the last few months you didn't give up on me like other people did. I know I want to be with you. I can learn to be the woman you think you see when you look at me. Just say yes, please."

I looked into her eyes and saw sincerity. She took my hand. I drew a deep breath and closed my eyes, and I said yes. She grinned and pulled me toward her, but I was afraid. There was a tiny voice, almost a loud whisper inside my head that asked, *Are you sure? Will she leave you abruptly again?* I decided that we would take it one day at a time. After all, that was all we could do.

"What's on your mind?" she asked.

I just sat there, staring straight ahead.

"Sadira, what is it? What are you feeling?"

"I want to make love to you."

She looked shocked, frightened even, as if she hadn't realized that I would want more from her. Jessie was silent. I looked her directly in the eyes. She slowly came closer, and hugged me.

"I'm scared," she said softly. "It's been a long time since I've completely given myself to someone."

"You don't have to be afraid, Jessie." I kissed her lips.

"But..."

"Shh. I promise I won't hurt you."

She looked at me with her begging eyes. They looked more gray than blue that night.

"Please, give me you," I said, climbing on top of her. "Open up to me. Trust me." I kissed her on the cheek, then her neck.

Jessie relaxed, opening her legs. She hugged me.

"I've wanted you for so long," I whispered, then unbuttoned her shirt. She was wearing a sky blue lace bra. I kissed down her stomach, smelling traces of the perfume she was wearing. She ran her hands through my hair then moved them to my shoulders. I kissed up and down both her sides, then slid my right hand behind her to unfasten her bra. She sat up to take both her shirt and bra off. I smiled and she returned a smile of her own.

I unzipped her pants and pulled them off. Her panties matched her bra. *Damn, she's sexy.*

"Take your clothes off," she said, finally relaxed and ready.

I undressed then looked at her from head to toe before locking eyes with her. A strange but wonderful feeling filled me. As we stared into each other's eyes, it felt as though we were mentally connected. Our emotions and thoughts were tangled within each other. I could feel how badly she wanted to have and believe in me. It was a chemistry that's hard to explain accurately without sounding crazy— like her mind and soul was on display to me. I could feel her mix of fear and excitement. *I only want to love you,* I thought and she smiled. I didn't say anything, but it was as if she knew what I was thinking. The sensations were incredible, intensifying my want for her.

Just as I was about to move closer, Jessie pulled me on toward her. I kissed her everywhere, sucking and licking her breasts. I took her panties off before lying on top of her. We kissed hungrily, feeding off each other's desire. She ran her hands up and down my back. We rolled over, still kissing so that she was on top of me. I thrust my body up into hers. She moaned. It felt like we were kissing for hours. Rolling over, alternating the top position, she ended up riding me until I climaxed. Shortly after, she did too.

She lay in my arms afterwards. I kissed her on the forehead. We didn't do half the things I'd imagined and fantasized doing on our first time, but it didn't matter. Never in my life did I have to work so hard to be intimate with someone. I would have been highly disappointed if it *wasn't* pure ecstasy. There was a connection established between us that made it the best experience I'd ever had. More mental and emotional than physical, Jessie fulfilled me in a way that no one had ever done, nor I think, ever could. She was worth the wait.

It was a cold and damn near frigid morning after Jessie and I became a couple. I woke up from an all night spoon position smiling and moving briskly. I thought about the fact that we didn't talk about our sexual history or past partners. I knew that it was irresponsible to do so and could only hope that I wouldn't have to worry about anything and not make that mistake with anyone else. I didn't even know how to bring the subject up *after* we'd already had sex and not offend her. I decided not to, believing with all my heart that nothing would go wrong.

It took me less than 30 minutes to shower and get dressed. She dropped me off at the subway station. My workday went by fast, and I spoke with Jessie once before finishing my shift at the radio station. It was New Year's Eve and I was glowing. I was looking forward to spending the evening with her.

When I got home from the station, I stretched out on my bed under indigo sheets and a thick navy comforter. Jessie and I made plans to meet up at a club in Lower Manhattan called M12 where her friend Janae was throwing a party so I wanted to get a nap before. I drifted into a quiet sleep. In a dream I saw a woman with a toast-brown complexion, natural hair, and striking green eyes. She was wearing a lab coat with white pants and saying something, but she was too far away for me to understand what she was saying. I didn't know if she could see me, or where I was. I assumed it was a hospital though it didn't look like one. She wasn't the only one wearing a lab coat, but she stood out. Just as my eyes met hers and she smiled, my phone rang and woke me out of the dream.

"Hey, sis," Khedara said.

"What's up?"

"Why are you asleep this early?"

"I'm tired as hell. What's up?"

"Well, you never told me what happened with you and that girl."

"Who? Oh, Jessie. We're a couple now."

"How did that happen? The last time you talked about her she was popping in and out like a damn jack-in-the box? Sadira, I remember you saying she was pretty and that better not be the reason you're taking her shit."

"No, and she's not that bad, plus we're getting along fine now."

"Okay, if you say so. But anyway, go back to sleep. We can talk later."

"All right, bye."

"Later," I said and went back to sleep.

I woke up an hour later hour to get dressed. I wore a tan turtleneck, black pants and shoes. Jessie and I agreed to meet at M12 at

9:30. Janae threw a good party, and was a pretty cool person. Jessie did get drunk though. I ended up having to ride all the way to Queens to see her home safely. I took the next day off work and we lounged around her place for half the day before I went home. She called me before I even got home to ask about going to an open mic session at Karma.

"Sure," I said. I signed in online to check my e-mail before showering, got dressed and went back out to meet her. It was really cold outside that night so everybody who stepped out to smoke huddled up together trying to get a quick pull in before going back inside the club. Jessie and I were waiting in line to get in, and as the smokers smoked, they complained.

"You know what?" the bouncer said. "Fuck Nicorette Gum and those stinking ass patches, if you really want to quit smoking, stay out here for longer than five minutes and you won't want to smoke for another month!"

I could hear the hip-hop music coming from downstairs in the club as I dug my hands in my pockets to keep them warm.

"I swear I saw two people frozen in place trying to cross the street today," I heard someone else say. "I'm telling you, a dog was trying to take a leak on a hydrant and got stuck with his leg up for about twelve minutes until animal rescue came."

Yeah right. I laughed. But it was really cold so as soon as we got through the line we went straight inside and didn't come back out until it was time to go home. It was a decent sized place. I was disappointed that they didn't have a coat check, and surprised that there was a bathroom attendant. The lights were really dim except for the stage and there were candles on the tables.

I decided to go on stage as S. Cooper and read a piece on the theme "self-determination" instead of erotica. The crowd felt it just the same, especially my repetition of the phrase, *As I press on and take life head-on/I move forward by these four words: I can do anything.* Jessie really liked it, as a matter of fact, as I stepped off the stage, she walked up to me and gave me a hug in front of everyone. *She's coming around,* I thought. I gave her a quick kiss on the cheek, and she rubbed my back.

"Do you want a drink?" I asked her during the intermission

"Yeah, Red Devil, thanks."

It took me ten minutes just to get through to the bar. When I returned with her drink Jessie tried to lead me to the dance floor.

Uh oh, I thought. "I don't dance, Jessie."

"What?"

"I don't know how to dance."

"Whatever," she said and pulled me on the dance floor anyway. *Shit!* Funny, because though I loved music and worked at a radio station and a club, I absolutely hated dancing. I never felt like I was good at it and didn't want to make a fool of myself. But since it was Jessie, I gave in and decided to try. Plus I didn't want to pass up a chance to feel her grinding up against me. *I might not see her for another week or two after tonight.*

If ever there was a person who danced provocatively, her name was Jessie. She kept it simple at first so I could follow, but once Beyonce's "Baby Boy" came on she melted into the rhythm of the music. Anyone who could see us looked at the way her hips swayed enticingly. Jessie had a sly seductive way of moving. Turning to face me, she came close enough to kiss but teasingly looked directly into my eyes before backing me up against a wall. I tried not to let my mind wander, but all I could think about was sleeping with her again. Something about the way she moved mesmerized me, it almost put me in a trance. We danced to a few more songs before another femme, a lesbian who is more feminine than butch, asked if me she could dance with Jessie. "Sure," I said. Damn, the two of them dancing was a nice sight too. I don't consider myself femme or butch. I can be either or, and I hate to be labeled. My problem within the lesbian community is that people automatically label each other based on clothing. Most of the time I dress more masculine just so I don't have to deal with butches, plus I attract more femmes. I don't always feel like dressing that way though.

Four hours later at home my clock radio scared the hell out of me. I must have turned it up loud to make sure I didn't sleep through it. After hitting the snooze button two more times I got up and took a warm shower before getting dressed in three layers to brave the brutally cold morning. It's funny because when I first walked out of my building I thought, *it's not that bad.* Then I took a few steps and the wind hit me so hard I wanted to sprint to the subway station. It was seven degrees with a negative twelve windchill.

I was twenty minutes late to work thanks to police activity in the subway. By the time I got there the morning show host, Devonte, was already in the middle of his show. I could hear him going into a commercial break.

As I was walked by the DJ booth I heard, "Sadira, wait up, nigga!"

"Devonte, how many times do I have to tell you to stop talking to me like one of your cronies?"

"Oh, come on, you know it's all love," he said with a big smile. "You *are* like one of the fellas, and I mean that in a good way. No offense."

"None taken. What's up?"

"Well, my cousin, Tricia is coming up to visit for a week, and she likes cats like you do if you know what I mean."

"Devonte," I said, cutting him off. Sometimes he made it really hard to like him.

"Sorry, sorry. But, anyway, I was thinking I could introduce you to her, and maybe you could show her around circles that are familiar to the both of you. Hell, me, you, JD and her can even go out to a club or something. What do you think?" JD was the co-host of his morning show. She wasn't ghetto like him, but she was funny.

"Are you trying to hook me up, Devonte?"

"Please, I wouldn't want you in my family!"

"Shut up," I said and laughed.

"I'll ignore that. So will you take her out?"

"What's she like?" I surprised myself at how interested I was. "How old is she? Tell me about her."

Devonte smiled and shook his head approvingly at my obvious interest. I looked at my watch and noticed I was running late. "Devonte, I have to go, but call me later and we'll talk."

As I walked to the subway, I found myself smiling at our conversation. I didn't know why, but I was looking forward to his call and hearing about his cousin.

That night when I left my 2nd job a slight drizzle began to fall. I probably wouldn't be riding the bus late at night much longer since I was thinking of quitting bartending because it made me feel too tired, and I really didn't *need* the money anyway. It wasn't until I got in from the club that I realized I missed Devonte's call. I wondered why I was so interested in his cousin. Things seemed to finally be falling in place with Jessie, but a part of me honestly wanted to meet this girl. Was I wrong? After working so hard to get close to Jessie, I hoped I wouldn't do anything stupid to mess it up.

Chapter 4

The next morning I routinely got dressed and went to work, barely remembering any details from the time I left my house to arriving at the station. Devonte finally told me about Tricia. She was two years younger than me and would be visiting soon for a mix of vacationing and job hunting. She had interviews at the corporate offices of Chase Bank, Citigroup, and Bank of America. A part of me was definitely looking forward to meeting her.

Meanwhile, throughout January Jessie started acting like her old self, fading in and out of my life. It aggravated me to no end, but I could not hate her for it. My heart wouldn't let me. After decreasing our phone calls to almost none, Jessie inspired something in me. I wasn't quite sure what emotions it triggered, but think it was more a blend of emotions that poured from me as I spread my battered feelings on pages before typing and e-mailing them to her.

Either I'm super Sadira, am learning a lesson in patience, or am just plain dumb. Which one is it? We had been dating for a while now, and I'd surely proven that I wasn't a lunatic who would show up at her job in house slippers and church socks with a bumblebee jacket on. *I don't understand what's wrong, Jessie. Why are you the way you are? You come and you go. Do you like me or just my gestures? I'm asking because I can't do this anymore. I can't just take you jumping on my heart as if it were squares drawn on the sidewalk with chalk. I'm being honest. No games, no drama. What's going on?*

I was on the edge for three days before I got a response from her. *I need to make this clear,* she wrote. *I appreciate all you do, every sweet gesture, every thought, every sweet word that comes from your lips. If you were to do none of these things, I would still like you. I like your persona above all. I like the way you think, how you live, how you inspire me without any actual attempt to be different. I'm sorry that I keep hurting you. I have so many flaws in the relationships and thought that I could fix them if I stopped running from one, but apparently I was wrong. Before you came along I told myself that I would take time off from dating to brush off all of my ill feelings toward women, but I went against that to be with you. And as I sit and think, I conclude that perhaps we do need time apart because the last thing I want to do is cause you pain...again.*

After we communicated a few more times through e-mail, I wrote her one last real letter and mailed it along with a cassette tape. The titles of the songs incorporated what I had to say, and that was it.

Khedara called me that night to catch up. We hadn't been talking nearly as much as usual. I hoped that would change just as soon as I quit my part-time job.

Two more days went by before Jessie called and left a message. She had indeed received the letter and tape in the mail, and her voice sounded like she was glowing.

"It was absolutely impeccable and so sweet of you, my God, Sadira, what are you doing to me? You are challenging my notion that all women do is hurt and abuse. Listening to the music and reading your words brought tears to my eyes. I don't know what to do or say right now. I just know that I'm very happy and smiling because of you."

I didn't return her call immediately, but I soon broke down and called her. I missed her. The cycle began again.

This time Jessie and I progressed to a point of seeing each other every day. Sometimes I spent the night at her place. I surprised her by having flowers sent to her job. And she actually followed through on most of our lunch dates. She made plans to introduce me to her mother. I even spoke to Jessie's mom on the phone one day while I was at her place. I began to become hopeful about finally having a normal relationship with her, but those hopes were soon shattered when she slowed down the phone calls and visits again.

Goddamn her! I didn't know how much more I could take. Fed up, I decided to talk to her. Both Jessie's home and cell phones went to voice mail when I called. I waited a few minutes, and then tried again. No answer, just five rings before voice mail. I waited a little while longer before I logged online, and there she was.

I typed *Jessie* but there was no response. *Look, we need to talk, but I don't want to do it online. I'm not in the mood to chase you, so when you see this I suggest you call immediately or discontinue calling altogether.* With that I finished and logged off. I realized there was so much anger buried deep inside me toward her. Not long after I logged off the Internet, my phone rang.

"Sadira, what's wrong?" Jessie asked, skipping the hellos.

"I can't do this anymore."

"What are you saying?"

I sighed. "Jessie, I'm saying that I'm not happy with you. As a matter of fact, I'm pissed. I'm not a fucking convenience store, Jessie. You can't just keep coming in and out of my life as you please without regard to my feelings."

She was quiet.

"For six months I've been trying to adjust to you. Six months, Jessie. I've been trying only to respond to the good in you, but I feel like I need a magnifying glass to find it."

"But Sadira..." Her voice trailed off into silence.

"I feel like we should go our separate ways."

"No."

"Yes! Jessie, you just don't get it, do you? How much god damned time and energy do you think I have to spend on you? Do you *ever* think of anyone but yourself? You're selfish, and I really don't think you give a shit about me."

"I'm sorry."

"We've had some fun and Lord knows I've given all I could to you in an effort to make this work, but maybe love isn't meant to be for us. I thought you were worth having because you were so hard to get. I was wrong. We should stop this dysfunctional relationship now. I'll go my way, and you need to go yours."

"I don't want you to go. You said you'd always be there for me." I heard her trying to mask the pain in her voice.

"I did say that, didn't I? I blame myself for thinking you were better than you actually are."

She sighed.

"Jessie?"

"Yes?"

"It's over. I have to go now," I hung up before she could respond or hear me cry.

Chapter 5

I made a few more changes in February, including quitting my part-time job at the club. I also went to see my doctor to make sure I had a clean bill of health. With plenty of newfound free time I decided to volunteer and also take my mind off of missing Jessie. I needed to get over her quickly. I also wanted to meet more women like myself for friendship purposes. Another relationship was not on my agenda.

Tricia was supposed to be in town, and I knew Devonte would be calling any day about our going out at night. It was a Friday night, but I hadn't gone to work that day because I had a doctor and dentist appointment. There was something about the day that made me unable to be in anything but a good mood. I'd done a little shopping and pampered myself after my medical visits with a manicure, pedicure, facial, massage and getting my hair relaxed and styled. I felt flawless. A few minutes after seven o'clock, Devonte called.

"Hey, Devonte."

"What's up, Sadira?"

"Relaxing."

"Cool. Well, my cousin is here, and I'm clear for tonight. I was thinking we could all go out first, and if you want to take her somewhere afterwards, then feel free to do so. That's if you two hit it off, but I think you will. As a matter of fact, hold on. Let me get JD on the other line."

"All right." It seemed like he had everything worked out already and just needed a "yes" from both JD and me. It had been a while since I had hung out with them.

"Sadira?" said Devonte coming back on the line.

"Yes."

"I'm here," JD said. What do you want to do tonight?"

"I was thinking dinner and drinks," he said, "if that's okay with you two."

"Where at, Devonte?" I asked.

"Virgil's or something, I don't know."

"What does your cousin want to eat?" JD asked him.

"I don't know."

"How about asking her, Devonte," I said.

"Yeah, yeah." I heard him then asking Tricia what she wanted.

"Okay, it looks like we're going to be in your neck of the woods, Sadira. She wants to go to Sylvia's to see what all the hype is about."

I smiled. "Is that okay with you, JD?"

"I'm all for it," she said.

"All right," said Devonte. "How about we meet up there at about 8:30? And then afterwards we can hit one of the comedy clubs on the East Side or split up, whatever. We'll decide after we eat."

I said, "Sounds like a plan."

"I'll be there," JD added.

We all said goodbye and hung up. For a moment I started to feel a shortness of breath, as if I were on the verge of an asthma attack. I reached into my nightstand for my inhaler. Moments later, I felt fine again. I hadn't had an attack in a long time and surely didn't want one on that night.

I lived less than fifteen minutes away from Sylvia's so there was no need to rush. I wasn't sure what to expect of Tricia since I hadn't actually talked to her, but if she was anything like Devonte she'd fit right in with JD and we'd be laughing all night. If she was attractive and attracted to me, well, we'd see. I was feeling a bit naughty.

When I entered Sylvia's, I recognized JD and Devonte with his shining baldhead immediately, but when I looked to his right I was taken aback. *That's Tricia? Wow!* Devonte nodded in my direction, and I caught Tricia giving me a look up and down.

"What's up, Sadira?" JD said when I got to the table.

"Hey, JD."

"Sadira, how come you live the closest, but got here last?"

"Shut up, Devonte. I might have gotten here last, but I'm not late."
Tricia cleared her throat.

"Oh," Devonte said. "Sadira, this is my cousin, Tricia. Tricia, this
is my co-worker and homeboy all-in-one, Sadira."

I gave him a nasty look for his "homeboy" remark, and then
reached out to shake Tricia's hand.

"Nice to meet you," I said to her.

She smiled. "It's nice to meet you too."

I let go of her hand slowly. It was quiet before Devonte broke the
silence. "Go on and sit down, Sadira, I'm hungry."

I didn't say anything. My eyes locked on Tricia's as I sat down.
He and Tricia were on one side with me and JD on the other. I was
directly opposite Devonte, but Tricia also faced me at an angle.

"Sadira, what are you going to have? The salmon cakes? I know
you want something like that." Devonte chuckled.

"Be quiet, you're not funny. Okay," I said laughing, "you are
funny, but I don't eat salmon."

"You might not eat salmon, but you damn sure eat fish. Go ahead
and add some tartar sauce to your order."

I kicked him under the table.

"Okay," said JD, breaking the back and forth between Devonte and
me. "I want chicken."

"Oh, Sadira," Devonte said, "I know you're not taking this
personal. It's all love, I'm sorry."

"It's cool. You're ignorant and can't help yourself."

Tricia laughed, then excused herself to go to the ladies room. Her
smile was very inviting. She was slim, with a smooth cocoa-brown
complexion, long straight hair, and deep, dark intriguing eyes. Dressed in
sexy heels, slim low-rise bootcut jeans, and a pea green tank top, she
reminded me of Jessie in a weird sort of way. A silk scarf was around her
waist rather than a traditional belt. Her skin looked perfect. We all ate
and had a good time. Tricia still looked good when she bundled up in her
tweed blazer. Her chandelier earrings matched her tank top. It was still
fairly early when we were ready to leave, so we decided to go to a comedy
club together. Bad idea. The acts there sucked, and JD complained that
she was ready to go to sleep. We tried another club, but it wasn't any
better. It was already going on 1:30 in the morning.

"JD," Devonte said, "why don't you take a cab home, instead of the subway."

"Man, do you know how much a cab from here to Brooklyn is going to cost me? The subway is just fine."

"Well, we can share a cab. I don't want you to go home by yourself."

"I'm not really tired," said Tricia. She looked at me. "Are you?"

"Me?"

"Yes, you," she said, then smiled.

"No, I'm not…" I began, but Devonte cut me off.

"Wait a minute, what is going on here?" he said and smirked. "Young lady, did I ask you if you were tired?"

Tricia looked him up and down as if to say *whatever, you're not my father*, "Devonte, seriously, I'm not tired and I really want to see New York."

"So what are you saying?"

"I'm saying I want to see the city."

"With who?" he asked.

Tricia sighed. "Why are you acting like I'm sixteen years old? The only thing I need to know is if Sadira would be kind enough to show me some things tonight and if you, Devonte, trust her to get me back to your place."

"I guess she told you," JD told Devonte and laughed.

He turned to me. "Sadira, do you mind?"

"No, of course not. It would be my pleasure."

"Well, I guess it's decided then. JD, I'll see you home safely." He turned to me. "Sadira, let me give you my address. I know you have my cell phone number."

"Okay, but if I take her to a club, we probably won't leave until it closes and then get some breakfast."

"Whatever, just keep in contact with me and take care of my cousin, chump."

"Relax, she's in good hands."

"Devonte, I have a couple of DVD's I haven't watched yet," JD said. "If I don't fall asleep in the cab, you can come home with me and watch them. That's only if you want to though."

Did JD just invite Devonte back to her place? Whoa. He gave her a look that said the same thing I was thinking. No one spoke for a few seconds.

"That's sounds fine to me," he finally said. "So, Sadira, do you have any idea where you're going?"

"It depends."

"On what?"

"On what it is Tricia really wants to see tonight. I mean, if she wants to go to a club, though I don't care for them that much, we can do that. If not, we can walk around the Times Square, or the Village, or go to a jazz spot, or something else. She's the guest, so whatever she wants is fine with me."

"How about a club for a little while and then the Village?" said Tricia.

"Not a problem," I said. "The only thing I can think of on a Friday night is a spot called Escuelita's. I've never been there before, but I've heard a lot about it. We can start there. Devonte, I think it's around 34th and 8[th,], but don't worry. You and JD go on home. We'll be fine."

We said our goodbyes and went our separate ways. I looked at my watch. It was 1:48 a.m.

"Tricia, we can take a cab over there, or the bus if you want to see stuff on the way."

"How far are we by bus?"

"Maybe twenty minutes or so."

"The bus is all right with me then. I'm trying to do things I normally wouldn't do. Taking the bus is definitely one of them."

"Oh, I see," I said as we began walking. "What kind of car do you have back home?"

"A Mitsubishi Eclipse."

"Oh, yeah? I can remember how bad I wanted one of those when I was in high school. But then they changed the body style to that spider stuff, and I didn't really care for it."

"Well, I have the Spider. It's a forest green convertible. It was a gift."

"Damn, I don't know anybody who ever got a car for a gift."

"Yeah, my parents bought it for me when I got my bachelor's, so I could get rid of the jalopy I was driving. They were real proud of me for finishing school so early."

"What jalopy was that? And how old were you when you graduated?" I asked her as the bus pulled up. I dipped my Metrocard twice to take care of both her fare and mine.

"Ugh, I forget the name of it right now, but it looked ugly and was shaped like a boiled egg. I think it was a Ford. I hated that damn car. Anyway, I finished high school when I was seventeen, but I was also taking college courses at the same time so I finished undergrad in three years instead of four, when I was 20. I just got my Masters."

"Wow. That's impressive." I motioned for her to slide into a seat. "I took a slightly different route, joining the Air Force after graduating high school. That's when I bought my first car, a Nissan Sentra. I sold it when I got out and haven't bought another one since. I really don't need one here, but when I move I'll lease a Benz or something."

"A Benz, huh? What did you do in the Air Force?"

"I was an audio and lighting engineer for the military band, and, yes, I'm in love with the CLK Benz. It's sexy."

She laughed. "The *car* is sexy?"

"Of course, like other things I see here tonight."

"Oh," she said and looked at me. "I see some attractive things myself."

We were quiet for a moment, both smiling inside at our forwardness. "Oh, I may as well warn you now." I told her. "I'm not much of a dancer. So you go right ahead and enjoy yourself. I'll be at the bar or a table or something."

"Please, you have to give me at least one dance."

"I'm not good at it."

"You mean to tell me you don't have any rhythm?"

"No, I didn't say that. I have rhythm, but not on the dance floor." I watched her reaction but wasn't sure she picked up on my innuendo.

"Well, you can just hold me from behind and follow my lead. It's not that hard, and I'll keep it simple."

"Okay, then. But don't say I didn't warn you when I start stepping on your feet."

"You'll be behind me, so there will be no stepping on my feet."

"Cool. We're almost there."

"All right."

When we got off and I took her hand, she didn't pull away. In fact, she held mine firmly. There was no cover charge, which was great, so we moved through the line quickly.

After we checked our coats I asked her, "Do you want a drink?"

"No, thanks, but I might take you up on your offer later."

They were playing hip-hop, and I was about to go to stand up against the wall when Tricia pulled me onto the dance floor. *Damn, she danced almost as good as Jessie.* I sighed at the thought of Jessie before pushing her out of my mind.

I followed Tricia's lead and was a having a good time. I got tired after a while though and excused myself to go to the bar.

Tricia said, "I'll have that drink now."

"What do you want?"

"Long Island Iced-Tea."

"Okay, I'll be right back."

I got Tricia's drink and an Amaretto Sour for myself before I went back to her. A couple of women were checking me out. I smiled at them but made my way back to Tricia. When they changed the music to Spanish, then Spanish reggae, we both sat down. I felt tired. After ten minutes or so she was ready to dance again, but I told her to grab someone else because I wasn't dancing anymore. She grinned and said she wouldn't be gone long because her feet were also starting to hurt. While Tricia was gone, my mind drifted off to thoughts of Jessie. I wondered what she was doing at that moment. I think I had a mental association of her and nightclubs. For a second I thought I saw her face in the crowd, but it wasn't her. Did she miss me as much as I missed her? Did she cry? I really missed her despite what she put me through. *Something is wrong with me,* I thought. *Why did I…*

"I'm ready to go now if it's okay." Tricia's voice interrupted my thoughts. I hadn't even noticed when she walked up to me. I tried to shake off my incoming thoughts of Jessie. I could visualize her smile and blue eyes. *To hell with her, Sadira,* I told myself.

After we got our coats and went outside, I asked Tricia if she wanted to get breakfast or just go home.

"I could go for some food, but you look tired. I'm sorry, I'm a night owl."

"I'm a morning woman, but I can hang. It's not like I have to work today, so breakfast is fine. There's a diner not too far from here, and their food is decent."

"Okay, you lead and I'll follow."

"All right." I led the way four blocks down to the diner.

During breakfast, we talked and laughed. *I have to remember to thank Devonte for introducing us.* I thought. *Devonte, oh, my God, he went home with JD.* I was sure I'd know what happened between them when I got to work on Monday. I doubted they would sleep together. I just couldn't imagine it. All I could picture him with was a bottle of pimp juice on the nightstand next to a pack of Magnum condoms. Ugh. Then again, he did show a softer side of himself tonight. *Maybe he is romantic.*

After breakfast I asked Tricia, "Are you ready for me to take you home?"

She stared at me. "Yeah, I guess so. I'm pretty tired now."

"Okay." Just as I reached in my pocket for Devonte's address, I remembered that he was with JD.

"Do you have a key to Devonte's place?"

"No, actually, I don't."

I sighed. "Okay, then we have a little problem if he's with JD because you won't be able to get in."

"I didn't think about that," she said and looked at me.

"Hold on, let me call his cell to see if he is still with her."

"Okay."

I called Devonte, but his phone went straight to voice mail after the first ring. I waited a few minutes and tried again, but it still went to voice mail. I didn't know what to do. I mean, I knew what I could do, and even though I was attracted to her, I was trying to avoid bringing her back to my place. She was sexy, but I still didn't know her. I tried Devonte's cell again ten minutes later, but still got the voice mail. I tried JD's home number and got her. She said he'd gone home two hours before and gave me his home number. When I called, he answered half asleep. So much for Tricia going back to Harlem with me.

"He's at home," I said to Tricia after hanging up.

"Okay, well, I guess we know where I'm going."

"Yeah, we can take the subway closer and just take a cab to his house from the station. It's too late to be walking."

"All right."

We got on the Brooklyn bound train and within five minutes Tricia was asleep on my shoulder. We were in the middle car, and there were no other passengers. I put my arm around her and lay my head back, trying to stay awake to make sure we didn't miss our stop. The train slowed down as it came into President's Street station. I tried to wake Tricia up with a kiss on the forehead, but instead of waking her up, she snuggled closer to me. Her body was warm and had a hint of her perfume.

"Hey, Tricia, we're here," I whispered." I brushed her hair from her face.

"Hm?"

"It's time to get off the train."

"Oh, okay." She quickly stretched and sat up.

We got off the train and walked up to the street level where I hailed a Gypsy cab to Devonte's apartment. It took less then five minutes to get there. I didn't ring his bell immediately though. Despite the cold, I wanted to talk to Tricia just a little bit more before I made my trek back uptown. I saw burnt orange color creeping into the dark sky as the sun began slowly coming up.

"Thanks for taking me out tonight," Tricia said.

"My pleasure."

There was a brief moment of silence before I asked her, "What's your schedule like while you're here?"

"Well, tomorrow I'm free, and the next two days I have back to back job interviews. Nights and the weekend will be more of a vacation. I really just want to see the city and do new things."

"I can imagine."

"Are you busy tomorrow night?"

"Actually, I'm not. Do you want to go to another club or something?"

"Yes, if you don't mind. It's just that seeing a club with nothing with women trips me out."

"Okay, we can go to Lovergirl. It's pretty big and always jumping with two levels, all women."

"I'd like that."

"Well, listen, I better get going. It will take awhile to get back to Harlem from here, and I'm exhausted."

"Why don't I ask Devonte if you can take a nap here first?"

"It's okay. I'll make it."

"Maybe you should just lay down for a while. Are you sure?"

"Yeah."

"All right."

We looked directly into each other's eyes. Then she turned and pushed the bell. I reached out and touched her arm, and she turned back to face me. I leaned toward her and kissed her on the cheek. "Goodnight," I said. It was a soft, quick kiss, but when I pulled back, she pulled me forward and placed a slow, firm one on my lips. The sound of Devonte opening the door from the inside pulled us out of the moment.

"I'll see you tomorrow," she said and smiled.

"Yeah, call me."

"I'll do that, and you get home safe."

"I sure will."

"Bye." She walked in the door past Devonte, who had sleep written all over his face. He mumbled a thank you to me before turning around and going back inside.

I fixed my scarf under my jacket and pulled my collar up. The morning wind was razor sharp as I hurried to the subway. As soon as I settled into my seat on the train, I dozed off. An hour later I woke up just in time to hear the conductor call out 116th street. I exited the subway station into the morning light and hurried home to collapse on my familiar bed. I had a great night.

Chapter 6

The next day at four o'clock in the afternoon my phone woke me up.

The caller ID told me it was Khedara. "Hey, sis."

"What's up, girl?"

"Not much. I just woke up."

"Did you go out last night or something? It's kind of late to be just waking up."

"Yeah, I did. What's going on with you?"

"Girl, I have a date tonight, and I think he's normal!"

I laughed. I hadn't heard her mention dating in a while. "Oh, really? Where did you meet him?"

"We met at Jiffy Lube of all places. Last week I went there for an oil change and was just drawn to him. I could tell he was interested in me but afraid to speak, so I approached him. We clicked, and I gave him my phone number."

"You whore! *Jiffy Lube,* huh?" I laughed.

"Whatever. I'm not being picky anymore. I just want to find a good man. It doesn't hurt that he has a killer smile *and* can give a tune up."

"What's his name?"

"David… and he's very sexy. Wish me luck. I'm overdue for some dick."

"Khedara!"

"Not tonight, but still…" She paused. "No, I can't do that on a first date."

"Whatever."

"So what's up in your life?"

"Not much is new." I told her. "I'm playing tour guide part of this week for Devonte's cousin, Tricia."

"How's that fool doing and is his cousin straight?"

"He is still a ghetto country boy with bad table manners and, no, his cousin is not straight."

"Is that so? How old is she?"

"Twenty-five. She's legal."

"Uh huh. Are you attracted to her?"

"Hell, yes, she is definitely worthy of doing." I paused. "Mm hmm, she can get it."

"Well, damn, you're just like a dude, I swear." Khedara laughed. "You better not hurt her feelings."

"I wouldn't do that. I know how it feels to be hurt."

"All right. Listen, I have to run. I was just calling to chat for a minute. I'll let you know how my date with David went when I get home."

"I'm going out tonight, too."

"Okay, I'll call you in the morning then."

"Cool."

"Peace."

I got up, yawned, and stretched before walking to the bathroom to take a shower. Thirty minutes later I was listening to smooth jazz in the kitchen, making blueberry pancakes and scrambled eggs with cheese and ham. I was starving.

I managed to get two loads of laundry done as well as clean up my apartment before going to the cleaners and picking up some clothes that I'd left there. As I was walking back home, I felt my phone vibrate in my pocket, but I couldn't get to it before the call went to voice mail. From the number it had to be either Devonte, or Tricia calling from his phone. After I got in and hung my clothes up, I checked my messages and heard her voice. *Hey, Sadira it's Tricia. I hope you got home okay. I meant to call you earlier when I woke up, but I went out with Devonte. Anyway, give me a buzz at his house. I look forward to hearing from you. Bye.*

I picked up the phone to call her back, but it rang just as I was about to dial.

"Hello?"

"Sadira."

"Yes?"

"Sadira, it's me."

"Jessie?" I said surprised. "What is it?"

"How are you?"

"I'm fine," I said stiffly.

"Are you busy tonight?"

Here we go again. "As a matter of fact I am."

"Really busy, or just busy?"

She obviously wanted to see me. I wondered, *should I blow Tricia off for Jessie or not?* I wanted to see Jessie, but I didn't want play the fool again either. "I'm busy tonight, but I'm free on Monday."

"Okay, well. Do you want to check out a movie or something?"

I hesitated. "I don't know."

"Please, Sadira."

I paused, then said, "Sure." *Why doesn't my mouth follow my mind instead of my heart?* I knew I was making a mistake, but I proceeded anyway.

"All right, great," she said. I miss you, and it'll be good to see you again."

"Yeah," I said softly.

"Well, I'll let you go now. I'll call you tomorrow, okay?"

"Okay."

"Bye."

"Later."

Jessie was like fire and ice, one day hot and light, the next day cold and dark. I didn't want her to be gone, but I couldn't tolerate her being around only when she chose to be. The call dampened my mood a bit. Our break up was still fresh, and I couldn't lie to myself about not missing her because I did. Why did she have to make things so damn difficult for us? *The gift and the curse,* I thought. She'd perfected the art of creating in me an irreversible need and desire for her. That was the gift she had, a great strength for her, but a big pain for me.

My mind traveled back to an evening I'd spent with Jessie in a lounge. She teased me all night. I longed to kiss, hug, and hold her, but no more than a hug was what I was allowed. She seemed to take pleasure in seeing the yearning in my eyes. She said it was so strong and visible that it was cute. Was I a masochist to put up with it? After that night I began to think I should be checked out by a psychiatrist because I had to be crazy as hell to still talk to her.

I stayed in for the rest of the day, snacking and watching DVDs. It was 7:30 when I reached over for my phone to call Tricia. Though I was kind of comfy and sleepy, I wanted to see her.

Devonte answered after two rings. "This is D, talk to me."

"Hi, Devonte, it's Sadira."

"Oh, hey. What's up, man?"

"Not much. Is your cousin around?"

"Yeah, she's right here. Are you taking her to another club tonight?"

"If that's where she wants to go."

"Okay, hold on." Seconds later Tricia was on the phone.

"Hey, how are you?" I asked her.

"I'm fine, and you?"

"I'm feeling pretty good myself. Do you still want to go out tonight?"

"Yeah, if you're up to it. Hold on."

"Okay." I heard her moving, probably away from Devonte.

"All right, I'm back."

"Great."

"So are you taking me to a different type of club?"

"Yeah, we'll swing by the place called Lovergirl I told you about. I have to tell you it gets really crowded in there. Either I don't go until 3am, or I go at midnight and leave by 3:00. Tonight I'd rather go early. I can have you home by 4:00 so Devonte doesn't have a fit."

"Sounds good to me."

"Great. Do you want to meet earlier and walk around beforehand?"

"Sure, I'd like that." I wondered if she was smiling.

"Okay, Tricia. I'm going to take a shower and get dressed. By the time I do all that and get down to Crown Heights to pick you up it should be about 11:00. As a matter of fact, I just realized how late it is. We won't have much time to walk around before going to the club. But that's okay. Anyway, be ready in an hour or so, all right?"

"I will."

"Great, I'll see you soon."

When I left my house to go to Devonte's, a light snow was falling. "Oh hell no," I mumbled to myself. "The one night I'm not wearing my baseball cap it snows, isn't that a bitch."

I took the subway to the stop nearest him, then came up and flagged down a cab and told the driver where to go. "President St. between Nostrand and Rodgers Avenues."

"All right, which side of the street?" he asked in a foreign accent.

"I don't remember, but I'll point it out."

"Okay."

When I arrived at Devonte's place, Tricia answered the door wearing a sexy caramel brown spaghetti strap dress that embraced her hourglass figure. I looked at her from head to toe, feasting my eyes on every detail from her neatly arched eyebrows, flawless make-up and beautiful hair, one side of which was tucked behind her left ear revealing one of her small but striking earrings. Her delicate necklace looked expensive and hung gracefully around her neck. Tricia's dress looked as if it had been made for her body only. Though it stopped above her knees, my eyes traveled all the way down her smooth legs and muscular calves to her high-heeled shoes. *Damn,* I thought, *she is beyond sexy.*

"Hey," she said, sliding her hand against the back of my neck.

I walked inside and closed the door behind me. "Hi. Are you all ready to go? Where's Devonte?"

"Right here," he said peeking out from behind a door inside. He came forward half dressed. I never really looked closely at his build before, but through his undershirt I could tell he had a barrel chest and chiseled abs. His arms were very defined. A tattoo of a D was on his left arm. I didn't want to admit it to him that I thought he had a nice body, so I just smiled and nodded, but I know he knew what I was thinking.

He laughed.

"What?" I said.

"Nothing," he said, still laughing.

I persisted. "What are you laughing at?"

"I see that look in your eyes, girl. You want me, don't you?"

"Oh, shut the hell up, Devonte. I am *not* looking at you like that. Is that baby oil on your arms, man?" I laughed.

"Whatever." He looked at Tricia. "As you can see, good looks run in my family."

"Well, it sure as hell ran right over you!" Tricia laughed.

"You know you're lucky you're so little, or else I'd fight you like a man."

"Uh huh." I laughed.

"You're too small for me to find a decent place to hit you, that's all."

"Yeah, yeah, anyway. Tricia, are you ready?"

"Let me just get my coat."

"You'd better get two while you're in there." Devonte said. "I don't know who you think you are with that outfit you have on."

"Shut up," she told.

"Sadira, take care of my cousin and don't let any freaks get too close to her. And don't *you*, get too close to her either!"

"Oh, you be quiet, D."

Tricia came back out with a full-length black coat, carrying a pocket-sized umbrella.

"Bye, Devonte."

"Later and you two be safe, I'm serious."

"We will," I said. "See you later."

Snow was still falling lightly outside. It was a little after midnight by the time we arrived at the entrance of the club. Luckily the line was moving quickly. It's too bad I couldn't say the same for coat check, since we had to wait for almost 30 minutes to get through. Rap music blasted from the speakers upstairs. After finally checking our coats I lead Tricia to the lower level where Jay-Z's "Dirt Off Your Shoulder" was being pumped through the speakers. It wasn't completely full yet, but it was still early. We relaxed and took in the scene against the wall. Tricia did get me to dance for a while. Then we went to the bar to get some drinks.

I stopped dead in my tracks when I spotted Jessie dancing with some girl only a few feet away. At first she didn't notice me, but when she did and our eyes met, it felt strange. When whoever she was dancing with noticed Jessie being distracted by me, she pulled Jessie closer. That made me laugh inside. *Look at her in that bright ass banana yellow sweater and Timberlands.* I shook my head. *Where did Jessie find this lame ass chick?* I refused to admit to myself that it killed me to see Jessie with someone else. I bought a drink for Tricia and taking her hand, walked over to Jessie. *Maybe she didn't miss me,* I thought. Jessie continued to dance.

"What's up, Jess?" I said, trying to be casual.

"Hey," she said to me. It was clear that I was the last person she expected to see there. She knew how much I hated clubs.

When Tricia slid her arm around my waist, I pulled her closer. Jessie gave me a puzzled look, but said nothing.

"This is Tricia," I told her, trying to be nonchalant.

"Hi," Jessie said to her and smiled without an attitude. Her dance partner gave me an icy stare. She even nudged Jessie, but I got no introduction to find out who she was. *Fuck off big bird,* I thought. Jessie probably didn't even know her name. Or at least I hoped she didn't.

"I'll see you around, Jess," I said to her. "Have fun tonight."

"Yeah, you do the same."

"I will." I said and followed Tricia, who was pulling me back into the crowd of people.

"Your ex?" she asked as soon as we were away.

"Yeah."

"I see."

"She isn't rude, so don't worry about any drama tonight."

"Oh, I'm not. Besides, you're with me, and I already know what's going to happen tonight."

Taken aback by her directness, I almost dropped my drink. "You do?"

She came closer to me, backing me up against a wall, and used the tip of her tongue to trace my lips. I closed my eyes as she pressed against me and nestled her face in my neck. I felt her tongue, then a wet kiss ending with a soft bite. I opened my eyes and remembered where we were. One of Sean Paul's songs was playing, the crowd was getting thicker, the temperature was rising, and the strobe lights were on. We were in a tight little corner next to some speakers when Tricia's hand slid up my inner thigh. She bit my neck again and moaned. *Time to go,* I thought.

"I'm ready to leave, are you?" I said, almost out of breath. I quickly looked around to see if Jessie had seen what had just happened. A part of me secretly wanted to make her jealous. I don't know if she saw, but it was definitely time for us to leave!

"Yes, let's get out of here." she pulled me by the shirt.

She had one hell of a look in her eyes. I took a deep breath. As we walked upstairs to get our coats, questions floated through my mind. W*hat if she wants more than sex? What if she's clingy?*

"Sadira," she said, pulling me out of my thoughts.

"Huh?"

"You have the tickets for our coat check."

"Oh, yeah." I walked up to the counter and got our coats. After helping Tricia into hers, we walked toward the exit. It was still snowing, outside, but it wasn't the kind of snow that stuck, so it wasn't too messy, just slippery. I didn't want to deal with the subway so we walked over to 34th Street where I hailed a yellow taxi. I told the driver where to go and he started the meter.

In the back, Tricia put her head on my shoulder and placed her hand on my thigh.

"Sadira," she whispered.

"Yeah?"

"Listen, I'm an adult, okay? What happens tonight stays in the past after it's done. I'm not trying to mess up any flow you may have going with someone else. I only have one question."

"And what is that?" Her honesty made me feel more at ease.

"Are you in a committed relationship right now or just dating?"

"Just dating."

"Oh okay."

Kind of late for that question, I thought, but I didn't say anything. There was a naïve sincerity about Tricia that I liked. I wondered if I should ask her the same question, but I really didn't care. *Did that make me fucked up?* For the next few moments I thought about what she said. I appreciated her honesty, but I began to wonder if she did things like this on a regular basis. I realized that I hadn't asked her about her sexual history. Shit, that was the *last* thing I wanted to get into at that moment. I took a deep breath and swallowed. I was pissed. I didn't want to talk about possible STDs, but knew I had to.

Deciding to get it out of the way, I said, "Tricia, I think we should talk a little bit first."

"Okay."

I cleared my throat. "When was the last time you had sex?"

I saw the cab driver look back at us through the rear view mirror.

"About four months ago," she said without hesitation.

"With a man or a woman?"

"A woman. I've never been with a man."

"Really?"

"Yes, that's the truth. And you?"

"Me? I had sex about a month and a half ago, and it was with my ex-girlfriend, Jessie. I haven't been with a man in a very long time."

"So, um…" she began but stopped. "Have you been tested?"

"Absolutely. I'm squeaky clean and you?"

"I have, but I'll be honest with you. The test was only two weeks after my last encounter."

I was silent, then asked, "Why did you and the last person you were seeing break up? Was she bisexual?"

"She was starting to show signs of a stalker. And, no, she wasn't bi. You?"

The cab driver looked back at us again. I wasn't sure if he had a smirk on his face or not. Sometimes cabbies were on the phone or playing music. Not him though. We got a nosey one.

"Well, you met Jessie tonight, and we broke up because she had issues I could no longer deal with it. She wasn't bi either."

"Do you trust her enough to be honest with you?"

"I honestly do and don't think the reason she disappeared was for another woman. She has other problems."

"I see. But you had sex more recently than I did."

"I know, but she's clean." I turned to look her directly in the eyes. We sat locked in a stare that begged for each other's trust and honesty.

"Okay," I said and leaned over and kissed her quickly. All the talking was drying me up and killing the mood. When I moved her hand closer to my inner thighs, she moved closer and slowly kissed my neck. I turned and kissed her on the lips. She moaned, leaned back, and pulled me on top of her. The cab driver cleared his throat. She heard him and gave me a look as if to ask, *do you care about him?*

"Fuck him," I whispered.

"No, fuck me," she said, then kissed me again.

"Yeah, you want me to fuck you?" I whispered in her ear.

"Yes, Sadira," she said in a breathy voice. "Take me."

I slid my hand up her dress in between her legs. She was warm, wet, and ready to receive me.

"Hey," the cab driver said. "Hey!"

She giggled. I teased her clit with my thumb before sliding my finger inside and turned her giggle into a moan. She grabbed me. I kissed her shoulder and neck and dragged my tongue up to her ear lobe.

"Tell me you want me," I said.

"I want you, baby," she moaned. "Oh, Sadira. Yes, fuck me."

"Ladies!" said the cab driver again.

"Okay," I told him. I gave Tricia a few more slow strokes of my finger before pulling it out.

She laughed.

"Which side?" the driver asked. I was so damn busy trying to get some backseat love I didn't realize we were close to my place.

"The house will be farther down on the right hand side. It's the one with the white car in front of it."

He pulled up to the curb and shook his head. "27 dollars."

I gave him 30 dollars and waited for Tricia to fix her clothes. Then I helped her out of the car. As soon as we got inside, I pushed her up against the door. While she unbuckled my jeans, I unzipped her dress. Our heavy breathing and soft moans filled the room. It got hotter the more we kissed and groped each other. I only stopped to pull my sweater from over my head. *Damn, her body is nice!* I thought as I watched her slide out of her dress and shoes. Tricia wore a dark green lace bra and thong set. *I'm going to tear her ass up.*

"Come on," I said pulling her into my bedroom. On the way, I tore off my undershirt and it fell next to my sweater and belt, leaving a trail of clothes. Since I'd left my TV on the R&B channel, sensual music filled my bedroom.

"Lay down," I told her, then took off my pants. I turned the light off and climbed in bed beside her. I kissed her, this time on her shoulder and then up to her neck, tracing a small area up and down before getting fully on top of her. Then I moved over to the side of her neck and kissed it as if it were her lips, massaging her with strokes of pure lust with my tongue.

I breathed slowly and heavily as I closed my eyes and kissed all the way down her left arm into the palm of her hand. I sucked her fingers and kissed back up and over to her right side. I then did the same to that side before going back to her neck. I sucked it slowly, and gently bit it. Then I traced the lobe of her right ear with my tongue and kissed her cheeks, her forehead, the tip of her nose, and her lips. She moved her body upward into mine in response to my kissing. I felt her hands slide up my back and unfasten my bra. Later after more kissing and grinding she tugged my boxers to get them off.

"Touch me, baby," she moaned. "Give it to me good, Sadira."

"Turn around and lay down on your stomach," I commanded, and she obeyed.

I unfastened her bra and kissed down her sides and spine. That's when I felt myself slightly annoyed that I didn't give myself enough time to look at her ass in that thong before turning off the lights. *Damn,* I thought. *Oh well.* I felt the curves of her body as I kissed all the way down both legs and back up.

"Put your face down," I told her, then pulled her ass up closer to me. I kissed, sucked, and softly bit her cheeks as she moaned before I told her to turn back around. One by one I sucked her breasts alternatively while my hand caressed the other. I kissed down her stomach and sides and licked around her navel. I continued to kiss lower, while parting her thighs. She moaned and grabbed my shoulders. Before tasting the essence of her, I moved back up and pressed myself onto her at full length and began to move in a wave-like motion.

"Damn, Sadira."

"Hmm, you like the way I move, don't you?"

"Oh, yes. Take it, baby." She held on to my back as I began to move in rhythm with D'Angelo's "How Does It Feel" that was vibrating through the room. I continued that movement for a several minutes before I slowed to a stop and slid back down to her center. I traced the exterior of her lower lips with my tongue before giving her one long slow lick from her opening to her clit. I kept doing it up and down, slow, hard, intense. I parted her legs even more, tilted my head to the left, and sucked her clit. I flicked my tongue against it and then went back to sucking and licking it in a circular motion.

I kept it up for about 30 minutes until her legs began to shake in convulsions. I knew she was about to climax, but it was too soon. When I came up and thrusted hard with my clit against hers, Tricia matched my every move. Soon she had me on my back. The view of her riding on top of me made it hard to hold my orgasm, but I did. Her smooth cocoa-brown complexion, sitting above me with her head thrown back was beyond sexy. Although she kept brushing her hair out of her face, she didn't lose the rhythm. She moaned. I moaned. I grabbed the sheets to keeping from screaming since I was getting closer to climax. *Hold out, Sadira,* I told myself and focused on remaining in control. I pulled her toward to me so that her breasts were in my face. As I moved up to take one in my mouth, she slowed down. I followed her slowing pace from below until she was lying directly on top of me again. Sweat ran from our bodies like water.

"Sadira?" she asked.

"Yeah, baby?"

"How does it feel?"

"It feels good, Tricia."

"Does it?"

"Yes! Go faster, baby."

"Faster?"

"Yeah...Tricia...oh, shit. Tricia!"

Taking complete charge, she guided us both into multiple orgasms. She collapsed in my arms after it was over. I kissed her on the forehead. It was 5:30 in the morning, and we both fell asleep.

When I woke up two hours later to use the bathroom, I remembered to call Devonte and let him know everything was okay. It had slipped my mind before, but I didn't want him thinking something bad had happened to us.

"Hey, Devonte, it was too late to be going all the way down to Brooklyn, so Tricia's here with me. I'll bring her home later, okay?"

"All right."
"Later."

Chapter 7

I woke up with Tricia's head in between my legs. I thought it was a dream at first, but the more I moved my body upward into her mouth and she pleasured me, the more I knew it was real. Her hands moved up my stomach to my breasts as she stayed down on me. *Damn, this is a good way to wake up,* I thought as I looked down at her. She gazed up at me as she used the tip of her tongue to lick me up and down slowly. The sight drove me insane. She had the sexiest look in her eyes. *Look at this gorgeous woman going down on me* was my last thought before closing my eyes and letting myself be swept away.

Sliding her finger inside me while still pleasing me with her tongue, she brought me to a thunderous climax. After I released, we didn't move. She left her finger inside to feel my post orgasmic pulse while I lay still feeling good.

"Damn," I finally said. "God damn. Come up here, girl."

She licked her lips, smiled, and moved up to lay on top of me. I put my arm around her and pulled the covers over us. She moaned softly. "I love your pussy."

"Yeah?"

"Yes, I love it. The way it's shaped, the way it tastes and smells, mmm." she licked her lips and sighed. "The feel of your clit hardening against my tongue gets me so hot. I love the way you move up into my mouth. Whew shit, I better stop before we're at it again."

"Damn!" was all I could say as I stroked her hair.

It was 1:30 in the afternoon when my phone rang, pulling us out of our quiet comfort.

"Let me get that," I said, and she got off me so I could reach for the phone. It was Devonte.

"What's up?"

"Hey, Sadira. What time are you coming over?"

"Hmm, I don't know. I guess after we eat breakfast."

"Why y'all still asleep?"

"Devonte, don't start with me."

"Yeah, yeah. But for real, when are you coming because I have things to do and I promised Tricia I'd take her shopping today?"

"Wait, hold on." I turned to Tricia. "What time do you want to go home? Devonte says he's going to take you shopping."

"Whenever, as long as we eat first," she said. "I'm starving,"

"Do you want to go to a diner, or do you want me to cook for you?"

"You cook?"

"Yes."

"Then that's what I want," she said with a big smile. "Cook for me."

"All right."

I went back to the phone. "Devonte, we'll be there in about two hours. Is that good?"

"Yeah, that's fine. Just don't be late, Sadira."

"I won't."

"Okay, bye."

"See you later, man."

I got up and made French Toast and cheese omelets while Tricia freshened up in the bathroom. We talked over breakfast but not in depth. A lot of things were left unsaid, and I think that's the way we both wanted it. At least that's the way I wanted it.

"I enjoyed last night," she finally said after a few minutes of silence.

"Me too," I said softly and smiled.

"Yeah," she said, grazing her fork with the tip of her tongue and then inhaling with her eyes closed. "Umph," she said shaking her head.

"What?"

"It was damn good."

I laughed. "Yeah, you've got some skills with that tongue of yours. I'm not going to lie."

"You better not lie."

"No, I give credit where it's due."

"Well, thank you."

"Anytime."

"Anytime…really?"

"Mm hm," I said, and we both retreated to eating silently. After I got dressed, we left to take her home.

As we walked to the subway, I asked her, "When are you leaving town again?"

"Thursday afternoon."

"Hmm," I said and sighed. "Will I see you at least one more time?"

"Do you want to?"

"Yes."

"Well then, you can. Is there a day that you have free time after work?"

"Yes, probably Wednesday," I said, remembering that I was going out with Jessie on Monday. *Jessie.* I missed her. *I wonder what happened between her and Big Bird.*

"Okay, then come by Devonte's place and we can do something," Tricia said, bringing me back to our conversation.

"Sure thing."

We didn't speak much on the subway ride. As a matter of fact, with the string of evangelists, street musicians and peddlers moving through the cars, there was more than enough noise. When we got to Devonte's house, I didn't stay long.

"Why did your landlord spell her last name out in Christmas lights on your front lawn? Damn, Christmas is over." I asked him.

"I have no idea. The same reason the only lights on her car are Christmas lights. She's got red, blue, and green draped all around the rusty ass Cadillac symbol in the front, and it's cocked to the side. Those motherfuckers blink too."

I laughed.

"Stop laughing at her, man. She's chic." He laughed.

"Anyway, good looking out, Sadira," he said as I was leaving.

I got to work the next day just in time to catch a part of Devonte's show. It was call in for advice day, and Devonte and JD had a lot of questions to handle. Since my workload was heavy that morning, I didn't really pay attention until I heard one question coming from a female voice, "Is it a bad idea to sleep with your co-worker?"

"Absolutely," JD said, "it's a bad idea." I remembered them going home together on Friday.

"Oh come on, JD, as long as both of you handle it properly, it's not always bad."

"Mm, I guess you're right," she said and smiled at him.

They did it! Now I was sure.

Then I heard JD's say, "Next caller, what's your name and where are you calling from?"

"Hey, my name is Latoya, and I'm calling from Queens."

"Hello, Latoya, what's your question?"

"Well, my ex-husband's girlfriend keeps calling me, accusing me of still sleeping with him and threatening to come to my job to confront me."

"Did you sleep with him again?" JD asked.

"No."

"Okay, well, tell her not to bring any damn drama to your workplace, and if she persists, tell her to meet you in a park. Then proceed to beat the hell out of her with a pack of frozen hot dogs, okay?"

Devonte laughed. "You're a trip," he said.

"I learned from you," she said smiling. *Look at them in there looking in each other's eyes. Yuck!* I drifted away from the show back into my own world.

Snow was coming down quick and hard when I left work. It was a good thing my jacket had a hood because the flakes were falling fast. By the time I got home there was at least four inches on the ground.

I pealed off my wet clothes and changed into dry sweats before tending to anything else. There were two new numbers on my caller ID,

Devonte's cell and Jessie. I dialed into my voicemail unsure of what to expect.

"Hey, Sadira," said Devonte, "a friend of mine got the hook up on perfumes and colognes. Let me know what you want. Why buy *Cool Water* cologne full price when you can have *Cold Ass Rain* for five dollars? They smell almost the same. Just don't wear it everywhere because for some reason it attracts factory workers and scalawags. Call me back."

"Idiot!" I said and laughed out loud.

I smiled and shook my head as I pressed 9 to save the message and then listen to the time stamp of Jessie's call.

Hello, Sadira, she began. I heard her take a deep breath. *I have a secret to tell you. I have to admit that I actually find myself really missing you. Strangely and ironically enough, I miss you. Well, I just wanted to tell you that. Call me back. I'm looking forward to seeing you tonight. You should know who this is, but if you don't, it's Jessie, **not** the new girl.*

Damn. She *was* jealous. I hung up the phone not knowing how to feel. Should I have smiled at the fact she missed me or frowned at the way she ended the call? I didn't know. I smiled. *Maybe she did see us that night. Good!* Though I was slightly comforted by her jealousy, a large part of my initial fascination with her that was still inside of me seemed to break down every mental block I put up to prevent her reentry into my life.

After lying still and staring at the ceiling for a few minutes, I picked up the phone again and called Jessie.

She answered. "Hello?"

"Hey, Jessie, it's me."

"I know who it is. I'm glad you called."

I sensed her smiling on the other end of the phone. "Yeah, well, what's up? Are you ready to see me tonight?"

"Of course, I miss you."

I didn't say anything. I didn't want to give in so soon.

"So, do you want to see a movie tonight or what?"

"A movie sounds good. I heard about an independent film showing down in Chelsea about a 13-year-old assassin. I forget the name of it right now, but I can look it up."

"Okay, that's fine with me."

We didn't talk much longer, but we did agree on seeing the film and going out for a bite to eat afterwards. That night I decided to wear my hair out as opposed to under a baseball cap. It had finally stopped snowing. I was dressed in fitted jeans and an apple green sweater. I stopped quickly at one of the neighborhood nail shops to get my eyebrows waxed, then headed down to the subway to meet her where the film was being shown.

It was getting colder and I was getting annoyed waiting for Jessie at the theater because she was late as usual. But just as typical, I forgot about her tardiness as soon as I saw her approaching me. Before I could greet her with a hug, she kissed me. No "Hello," or "Sorry I kept you waiting" or anything like that. Jessie placed her left hand at the base of my neck and kissed me so full and hard that I almost lost my balance. My hands ventured down her back to her behind. She didn't stop me like she normally would have. Instead, she kissed me even more passionately. *Wow.*

When she finally slowed to a stop, she looked at me and smiled.

I shook my head in disbelief.

"Are you ready to go in?" I asked her.

"Sure." So we went inside.

Jessie unbuttoned her coat and she looked stunning as usual. Her hair was pulled back, and the blue in her shirt brought out the radiance of her eyes. We stopped to get the tickets, popcorn, and soda before going in.

The film was really good, especially the surprise ending. I hadn't heard of any of the actors, but it was definitely worth the money. Shortly after it started I felt Jessie's hand on my leg, so I placed mine on top of hers. She moved in closer to me. By the middle of the film I had my arm around her and kissed her on the forehead. I had a funny feeling inside, a confused one. Again, I didn't know what to do.

It was freezing when we walked back outside. The wind felt like it was slicing my face. "What do you want to do now?" I asked her.

"If it weren't a Monday night, I'd ask you if you wanted company, but I know what time you have to be up in the morning."

I was taken aback. *Who was this, and what happened to the stubborn ass, non-emotion showing Jessie?* I suddenly remembered that I'd just slept with Tricia the day before. I should have taken a bow at the prospect of having these two beautiful women in my bed back to back. My mind toyed with the thought of having both of them at the same time, one on the left, and one on the right. Damn!

"Sadira?"

"Huh?"

"I guess maybe we should just go home."

"Yeah, I guess so."

She looked at me in a weird way and smiled.

"What?" I asked.

"I miss you so much, Sadira."

The wind was getting stronger and colder. I didn't respond to her statement, but I did take her hand as we walked to the corner.

"Did you take the train all the way in or did you drive?" I asked Jessie.

"I took the subway from the Jamaica Station."

"Okay." I told her and hailed a cab.

We didn't talk during the short ride. Instead, Jessie put her head on my shoulder and her hand on my knee. I felt a rush of feelings that I couldn't identify pass through me and realized she was weaving her way right back into my life and my heart wasn't going to stop her. When we got to the subway station I paid the driver and walked with her to wait for the E train.

I remembered back to the first day we met on the subway. God, Jessie was beautiful. Why did she have to make things so difficult by trying to control everything? I wished I could teach her once and for all that you can't have love without risking heartache, but I couldn't. She'd have to learn that on her own.

When she stared at me, I saw a miniature version of my face reflected on her blue-gray eyes.

"I'm sorry for fighting your advances while deep down wanting you. I'm sorry to keep you guessing at my feelings, but I truly have things to work out within myself. You should know that I do care a great deal about you."

"Well, Jessie, if you know that issues are there, all you have to do is work on them."

"I have so many flaws," she said softly and lowered her head.

I was at a loss for words as I saw a light from within the tunnel. Her train was approaching. We were both silent. She hugged me and let her lips slightly graze my neck. "I'll see you another time, Sadira. But until we see each other again, let us continue to look at ourselves." It was the same line that she ended all of her e-mails.

"Jess…" I began but she placed her index finger on my lips to silence me and turned to board her train. It hurt. I watched her get on the train and take a seat before heading back upstairs. But it was when the doors were closing I remembered that I had a CD for her. It was a copy of some of my live open mic performances that she'd missed and had begged me for. I foolishly stuck my hand to prohibit the doors from closing and went back to hand it to her. Just then the conductor announced that the train was being held in the station. I turned to get off.

"Oh, thanks," she said and smiled. "Wait," she said suddenly.

"What?"

"Do you really like her?"

I was silent. Less than a second later I heard the 3-1 melodic tone signaling closing doors.

"Never mind," she said quickly. Jessie, smiled nervously, and hurried me off the train.

.

Chapter 8

The next day I walked around dazed and confused. I spoke with Tricia that night, but my mind kept wandering. I did get to see her again before she left. We had dinner at a Lebanese restaurant in SoHo and talked about her time in New York, her thoughts on moving here, her interviews, and, of course, our personal lives and what would become of us. She got two job offers, one from Chase and the other from Citigroup. She wasn't sure of which company she would choose, but both positions were similar investment banking department jobs.

There truly was no "us," and luckily we both understood that. In the back of my mind I could already see my future playing out with Jessie. I felt it deeply, and though the rational part of me whispered no, the irrational part yelled *proceed*.

"Do you love her?" Tricia asked suddenly, breaking the silence as we walked to the subway station.

"Who?"

"Your ex."

I was silent for a moment. "No…or at least I don't think so."

"But you want to love her." It sounded more like a question than a statement.

"Yes, I think I do." *Did I love her or just the thought of loving her?* I wasn't sure.

"But why? Why would you want someone who hurts and confuses you?"

"I don't know. Sometimes I feel I have no choice. It's as if something is forcing us to be together. We're meant to be."

"Oh," she said softly. I wished I could take back the last part of my statement, but it was too late. It frightened me to think it was true.

We'd just passed through the turnstiles and were walking downstairs to the subway platform.

"Well, I don't know what to tell you in regards to that." she said. "I do, however, want to thank you for the time that you and I spent together. I don't regret a minute of it, and if I could do an instant replay, I would, even knowing what I know now about your feelings."

"Are you going to stay in contact with me?"

"Would you like me to?"

"Yes." The sound from the oncoming train got louder.

"Then I will." She smiled.

"Thank you." *Why couldn't all women be as easy to communicate with as Tricia?*

We got on the Brooklyn-bound train heading south so I could make sure she got home safely. It would be the last time I saw her before she left, and I knew I would miss her, not terribly, but a little bit. She was sweet, at least what I knew of her.

The days after Tricia left melted into weeks. I missed her more than I thought at first, but I buried those feelings inside of me. We chatted a few times on the phone, but the conversations became less and less frequent as Jessie and I drifted toward each other again. Jessie and I talked on the phone plus our old ways of e-mailing each other came back, and we even went out a few times.

It was March and still very cold. I'd spoken to Khedara and updated her on the events of my personal life. She advised me to have another person in my life in addition to Jessie and not commit to either of them until I was sure they were the person I wanted to be with. I didn't have anyone else at the moment, but there were plenty of beautiful women in New York I could try to reach out to. All I had to do was put myself in a position where I'd be visible, and I tried to meet other women and form no-strings-attached relationships, but that ended up in a string of dates with people I couldn't connect with.

I either had to totally get over Jessie or make things work with her. It had been almost eight months off and on with her. And as more weeks dragged on I started to feel unloved, but this time I knew it was my own fault. I was in love with the prospect of being loved by Jessie and wished that she would just stop running and give us a try. She'd said more than a few times that she didn't know how to let go of her fear. I couldn't move on completely or stay without feeling cheated in some way. Yet I truly loved her despite it all. The burning desire I had for her led me to believe she was the one for me.

I felt trapped. By wanting Jessie I let a perfectly good woman, Tricia, get away. Later I'd learned that Tricia decided to move to New York and take the job at Chase. I called Tricia one day out of the blue, but she had company. Disappointment consumed me. I was hoping I could talk to her about my confused state.

"I'll call you back, Sadira," she had said and hung up.

She was in the city getting settled right at the time I was contemplating moving with Jessie. I sighed. Thoughts on giving up on Jessie diminished, and I tried to make it work.

At a late lunch after work with Devonte I told him about my problem. "Leave her alone," he said. "Leave both of them alone."

I sighed.

"Listen to me, girl," he said. "I know you and my cousin had a fling when she was here and that's okay with me, but I also know you're stuck on Jessie. Leave Tricia alone if you're going to be flip-flopping. If she ever got hurt by you, that would really fuck up our friendship. I don't want you to get hurt either, which is why I keep telling you to leave that cat-eyed Jessie heffa alone. She's selfish. She has issues and despite what you may think, she is *not* the one for you."

"It feels like she is," I said, taking a sip of water.

"Pain is what you feel. It hurts. That can't be right. You're making a mistake in your mind, Sadira. You don't love her. You just *want* to be loved so much it feels like you already are. Fuck that. Drop her ass." He turned and signaled the waiter.

I wanted to cry hearing his cold truth. It began to give me a headache. We got up and he paid the check.

"Don't get all soft and shit on me now either," Devonte said as if reading my mind.

I walked back to the station with him so we could talk a little while longer before I left.

"Wouldn't you rather have a harsh truth than a soft lie? I know you probably don't want to hear any more, but too bad. Let me tell you something, okay? I have plenty of ex-girlfriends that I still love to this day. I know I can't go back to them because it wouldn't be good for me. You gotta do what's best for you. Don't believe in that follow your heart shit. Find out where your heart wants to go and run it through your common sense. Then make a *rational* decision."

I smiled. "My god, you're silly."

"I'm right."

I nodded slowly but didn't say anything else. He had managed to walk me to my nearby bus stop, so we said our goodbyes. On the ride home I heard his advice over and over in my mind. On top of his words were my own notes to myself. I had the feeling I should let Jessie go, and I knew that was what was best for me. But the truth was my desire to be loved overpowered all my reasons for leaving. I decided to stay.

Chapter 9

After I'd made my resolution to make things work with Jessie, we had lots of long talks. For the next three months she still disappeared, but not frequently and not for long periods. Still, I expressed my disdain toward her actions and threatened to leave for good. When she did it again, after letting her back in, I left her without notice for two weeks. I dated a couple of times, but mostly just stayed to myself. It felt strange at first, taking myself to the movies, but it proved to be good for me. I gave myself what I wanted so badly from Jessie, undivided attention and a display of love. My leaving her worked because she never did it to me again. My leaving upset her, but she did not dare ask me where I went. I told her she needed to feel what I felt. She finally tried her best to make our relationship work.

A couple of months had past and one night at the beach, Jessie told me, "I have come up with the odd idea of letting you see the world through my eyes,"

"What do you mean?"

"Part of it is fear," she began, "fear of getting hurt. I am afraid of feeling warm tears rolling down my cheeks. I'm scared of the kind of heartbreak that makes a person want to curl up and die inside."

I was sitting next to her holding her hand as a couple walked by. For so long I'd wondered what her problem was, and now on this warm summer evening, she was finally giving it to me piece by piece.

"Sadira, please just listen and not say a word. I am nervous right now. I should be writing this in a journal, or telling it to a therapist, but something is telling me to start with you. Take in everything that I will share with you tonight. Please just be a friend and listen without judging."

I nodded yes and she continued.

"You know my biggest fear is being alone for the rest of my life, but it seems as if I keep aiding in that inevitable fate. I keep running away from you, though I know you are good for me. I want you to be with me, yet when you shower me with beautiful emotions I run away." She took a deep breath. "I feel trepidation that you are perhaps too good to be true. I retreat into myself. I won't let my heart be ravaged. I refuse."

She stopped as if she were about to cry, but she didn't. We sat and watched the waves lap against the sand. I let out a deep sigh.

"I'm sorry for hurting you," she said, turning to me. "I really am. I've been thinking about how I've acted all this time. It occurred to me that although I didn't purposely put you through pain, in my warped way I found a way to hurt you before you had a chance to hurt me. I've noticed that I repeat the same behavior over and over with woman after woman. I destroy them before they have the chance to destroy me. But then I had to ask myself with you, what if she has no intention of destroying me? What if her only goal was to love me and make me happy?" She fell silent and stared into the dark ocean.

Jessie leaned into me but remained hushed. I didn't know what to say, so I kept quiet. It was an odd ending to the evening, but that was all she told me about herself that night. We stayed out for another hour saying little before going home. Both in person and through e-mail she tried to explain to me and to herself why she was who she was.

I limit myself, she wrote in a handwritten letter. *I think it started when I was about eight. That was when my father left our family. He was truly my knight in shining armor regardless of how many times he beat my mother and eventually me, my sisters and brother. I loved him with every bit of innocence I had in me.*

Reading that, made my eyes tear up. That was about the same age my own life started falling apart. I took a deep breath and brought the letter closer to my face as if bringing Jessie closer to me to comfort her. *I had an unbound love for my father even though he left a lot. Whenever he came back I cherished his presence even more. I see myself a lot like him now although I never really got to know him. His repetitive disappearing acts have obviously rubbed off on me. Unfortunately my mother never corrected him. She never told him to stay gone. She loved him too much to do that, and she never said one bad word about him in front of me. He may have had other women on the side. As a matter of fact, I'm sure he did. The difference between him and me was that I never left you for anybody else. I left for myself.*

That time you left me forced me to take a hard look at myself in the mirror. I was afraid you would never come back. I asked myself just who did I think I was to leave you without notice and not expect a negative response when I got back. The majority of women I've dated left me. Some even told others to beware of me, but you stayed. I'm sorry I trampled your heart in my selfish confusion, but I thank you for not leaving. I appreciate you. It took you leaving me for my eyes to open and see exactly what I was doing to you. I want you to know that it hurt me to leave you just as much as it hurt you to be left. The more time I spent away from you, the more I realized that I was defeating the purpose of protecting my heart.

I am ready for you,
Jessie

"My god," I said aloud when I finished reading her letter. Of course, I was apprehensive about committing to her again, but I did, which lead me back to Miami. As much as I said I did not want to move back to my hometown, I did it anyway. Jessie got the opportunity to fill a management position if she was willing to relocate to Miami. We went back and forth on the pros and cons of moving and why I didn't want to go, but in the end we moved. The truth is that I loved her wholeheartedly and would have moved to Haiti if she really wanted me to.

Part II
18 Months Later
Miami, FL

Chapter 10

I know it may seem strange to make such a decision with a person who repeatedly flaked out on me, but I did. I took a chance, and it was good so far. I got a job as an office manager at an FM radio station in Ft. Lauderdale, and we bought a townhouse. I missed Devonte and JD terribly though. They threw a party for me at the station before I left, and we went out again that night. If I were ever in New York again, I'd definitely have to see them.

There wasn't a ghetto talk show host at the new station I worked at, and no one near as crazy as JD or Devonte. In fact, it was rather conservative and more of an easy listening station, but it was a job and the pay was good. I didn't expect to make the same salary I'd made in New York, but they came close to matching it. I also found a club that hosted open mic events, Avery's, and I occasionally went and did a poem or two. I created a small fan base with the spoken word crowd as well as made photography a new hobby, enrolling in a few classes. Life was good, and I liked being back in Florida.

Jessie and I had fun, and most of the time things went smoothly. For my first birthday there She surprised me by taking me on a cruise. It was the first time I'd been on one and had a wonderful time. She still hadn't learned how to cook, but that was okay. I knew enough about cooking to keep us alive, and if I didn't feel like being in the kitchen, we ordered out.

The period of domestic calm ended when a woman left a message for me on our message service.

"Come here, now!" Jessie yelled at me.

"What's with your attitude?"

"Listen," she said with one hand on her hip and the other pressing the speakerphone on. Jessie dialed into the voice mail service, and I heard, "I'm *going* to sleep with Sadira, Jessie. I know what she's missing at home and believe me I'm here to give it to her." Click.

"Who was that bitch, Sadira?" she said angrily.

I had absolutely no idea, but I braced myself because I knew a big argument was coming. She would hurl questions at me without giving me a chance to answer before firing the next one. Right about then my eyes started to glaze, and my ears filled with imaginary cotton. I could see the birds flying around outside through the window behind her. I had a taste for oranges. I spaced out.

"See this is what I'm talking about. You don't listen!"

"Huh?"

Bam! Right across my face she slapped me. "Who was that?"

"I don't know!"

"I'm not joking, Sadira. Who was that?"

"Baby, I don't know."

"How did she get our number?"

"I don't know." I wasn't sure I recognized the voice and couldn't think of who would leave that kind of message. Frustrated, I went to the kitchen.

"Where are you going? We're talking," she said. "Sadira!"

"Yes?"

"Really, what was that about?"

"For the last time, I don't know."

"So why would…"

"Lies. Prank calls, Jessie." I didn't want her to overanalyze the situation and give us both a headache looking for something that wasn't there. "Don't worry about it," I told her, standing at the kitchen counter cutting an orange in half. At the moment I didn't know if it was because my adrenaline was flowing or because of the intensity of her emotions that I wanted to defuse, but I felt a sudden urge to make love to her.

"Lies?" she asked softly.

"Absolutely." She looked directly into my eyes, searching for sincerity. "Go in the bedroom," I told her.

"What?"

"Go in the bedroom."

"No."

"Please?"

"No."

I hated when she did that. "All right, fine." I pulled a bowl out of the cupboard.

"What are you doing?"

"Making a fruit salad."

"May I have some?"

"Hell no."

"Why not?"

"Because I said so, punk. Get your own damn fruit. You must think you have a servant here." Unable to keep a smile off of my face, I put some grapes and strawberries in the bowl and hugged her. I ignored my desire to be intimate with her and relaxed instead. We spent the rest of the day inside since it rained all day and into the night.

The next day when Khedara called, I told her about the mystery phone call.

"So how are you two really doing?" she asked.

"Oh, everything is fine."

"Sadira?"

"What?"

"Don't lie to me."

"I'm not."

"When are you going to tell Jessie the truth?"

"The truth about what? I didn't do anything."

"I know, but I sense you've been unhappy for a while now. You don't want to get to the point where you *do* look elsewhere for attention. I know you're lying to yourself about being happy, but you can't fool me."

"It's not that I'm unhappy. I love Jessie."

"I don't doubt that you do."

"It's just that…" I paused and sighed. It was time to stop running from the truth. I wasn't fooling anyone, not even myself. "It's too late now," I told Khedara. "I can't expect her to change. I met her this way and decided to pursue her anyway."

"But…"

"I know. I don't feel appreciated. It feels one-sided. I don't want to leave, but I'm not sure if I should stay. I'm so confused."

"Just talk to her."

"What am I going to say?"

"Exactly what you just told me."

"It's too late. I just have to make things work."

"Don't make me come down to Miami and knock some sense into you. You're sounding like a punk right now, Sadira."

"I'm not a punk!"

"You're so darn soft, I swear. Woman up, Sadira."

"All right, all right, I'll talk to her."

"It's about goddamn time. Listen to your older sister."

"Whatever, you're only older than me by seven minutes."

"That's enough. Anyway, about the call, don't sweat it. Just be careful who you share your feelings with. You may have complained about something, and it was overheard and spread. You know how people gossip."

"I know."

"Look, sis, I have to go off and fire this damn girl now. Let me know how things turn out."

"Fire who?"

"My sorry ass assistant. I'll tell you about her later. Call me."

"Okay, I will."

Before I talked to Jessie I decided to go back and look at some things from our past, so I could see where I made mistakes. I didn't want to blame all of my unhappiness on her because I knew I had a role in it. There were things that I closed my eyes and ears to in the beginning.

I had a small box where I kept a lot of old e-mails and conversations between us. Feeling like Celie and Shug from "The Color Purple," I opened the box and pulled out letters. I read them over carefully, some parts out loud.

Just to let you know, I don't prefer one type of lesbian to another. You can be a stud or femme, I really don't care. I'm more interested in the person inside not what they feel more comfortable dressed in. It was good for me to hear her say that in the beginning. I was so tired of having to change to be somebody's perfect girl. Either they wanted me to look harder or more femme, or more this and less that, or whatever. I longed for someone who would accept me as I was, and Jessie did, but there was more that I definitely should have listened to though. Her flaws definitely outnumbered her assets. I continued to read.

I have a bad habit of keeping thoughts to myself even if it can be good towards a situation. You know I have issues. That's why I always tried to avoid relationships because I knew I had so many flaws that I wouldn't be able to make anyone happy. You have this tendency to make me feel so good inside. I am amazed by your ways of making me feel special, but I need you to be my friend. I need to clear my head and brush off all the stereotypes I have of women in general, shed all fears that still reside in me from past painful relationships.

But I was scared. I was afraid that if I gave her space, she might leave and not come back. I did try though. I tried to give her some space, but it just didn't work out. Would we have what we do now if I put my foot down? But what did we really have? I'm hurting, and she is oblivious. *Just how would she change now if I never said anything all this time?* I continued to sift through e-mails and instant message conversations that were now more than a year old. *I felt as though the more I spend time with you, the more I confuse and hurt you. It's not my style to say goodbye. I just disappear. I'm the type of person who people always end up wondering whatever happened to me, like a mystery or a ghost.*

I went through pages and pages of old conversations, some containing information I don't know how I overlooked or let slide. It's amazing how people can hear and see what they want to in the beginning stages of a relationship and then want their partner to change later. I made poor choices, judgments, and mistakes concerning Jessie, and now I had to fix them, if they were fixable. *I miss you Sadira, I really do,* she'd said. When I asked her what was it that she missed exactly, she said, *It's everything. You compliment me. Where I'm weak you shine. You make feel like life is worth living.* "Just talk to her," I heard my sister's voice say.

The sound of Jessie's jeep pulling in the driveway snatched me out of my thoughts, and I quickly put the letters away like a child caught peeking at Christmas presents. I looked up and mouthed, *God, help me,* and went to greet her. Just as Jessie entered the house, the phone rang.

I answered it. "Hello?"

"Hey, baby," a female voice whispered.

"Huh?"

Jessie dropped her bag at the door and looked directly at me. She must have seen my confused look.

"Are you still lonely?" the voice asked.

Jessie asked. "Who is that?"

"Who is this?" I asked but heard a click then the dial tone.

"What was that about?" Jessie wanted to know.

"I don't…I…I don't know," I heard myself stutter. *Oh shit.*

"Sadira!"

"Yes?" I hoped she wouldn't press it, but I knew she would.

"Who was that?"

"I have no idea. Jessie at least take your shoes off, sit down and unwind. I promise we're going to talk."

Ring.

"I'll answer that," said Jessie

I'm in for a long night.

She picked up the phone. "Hello? No, we're not interested." She hung up. "Damn telemarketers. Sadira, as soon as I settle in, we need to talk."

"I know, baby, I just said…"

"Because I need to know what's going on."

"Me too."

"I've been at work all day, so the last thing I want to come home to is drama."

"Jessie, relax."

"You hush," she said and went into the bathroom.

While she showered I pulled out some lasagna that I'd made the night before and heated it up so she could have it when she got out. After a shower and something in her stomach, I hoped she'd be calmer.

"Sadira!" she yelled from the bathroom.

"Yeah?"

"I forgot my towel. Could you hand me one, please?"

"Sure, hold on a sec." I went to the hall closet and took out a towel. "Here," I said when I opened the door. The bathroom was fogged up, and she stood naked in the middle of the mist with beads of water sliding down her body. We locked eyes, and I smiled. I hoped the night would be smooth, but I didn't know what to expect.

"Thanks," she said.

"No problem."

At the table I held Jessie's hand and said grace. "Dear God, we thank you for this food that we are about to receive. May it be nourishing to our bodies and provide energy for us to live life abundantly and with a pure heart, Amen."

I released her hand, and we both smiled. It had been second nature ever since our early dating days that one of us, usually me, said a prayer before eating, even in public.

"So how was work?" I asked.

"Awful. I got stuck in a traffic jam on the turnpike this morning for more than an hour, my heel broke, and other things went wrong, but it calmed down toward the end of the day."

"I see." Watching her eat a fork-full of lasagna, I took a deep breath, "Well, Jess, what I want to talk about is how I feel in our relationship."

She didn't say anything. Instead, she nodded, signaling me to continue.

Although I was nervous, I proceeded. "I don't know about the phone calls. All I can think of is maybe someone at the radio station overheard me on the phone with Khedara or something."

"Okay so, what is it you're feeling? Obviously you're unhappy."

"I feel like you take me for granted sometimes."

"How so?"

I took a sip of water. "Well, it's little things that I should have spoke up about a long time ago."

"Like what?"

"You just seem uninterested at times…like my job is a hobby or something. Or before we lived together, in our earlier days, I'd call you and you'd call me back a week later. You were too busy for lunch or to come hear me at open mic, stuff like that."

"Even though I was busy, I still listened to the CD's you gave me all the time. I was and still am interested in your creativity. How come you're bringing all this up now?"

"I didn't know how to say it before."

"Sadira, I'm sorry if you feel like I don't notice the things you do because I do. I know you work hard."

"I mean in the beginning when I was doing small things for you like taking you to the dinner and sending you e-cards. Sometimes I even felt you were unappreciative and inconsiderate. I didn't want to make a big deal because as far as the e-cards, I knew you received them. Jessie, you've always made more money than I do, yet I'm always doing nice things for you. What about me? We have a role-less relationship, so I don't want to hear that I'm doing what an aggressive or stud or whoever is supposed to do."

"I wasn't going to say that, but you make it seem like I've never done anything nice for you. What about your birthday?"

"Yes, for my last birthday you surprised me with a cruise, but what about just because? Or just asking about my job?"

Her face had no expression as she took in my words. She took a deep breath. "I'm sorry, Sadira." "I didn't know you felt this way."

"I know. You had no clue. I should have spoken up."

"Yes, you should have because I didn't know I was being insensitive. I thought you knew I appreciated you. So what do we do now?" She wiped her mouth with the napkin.

"I know you appreciate me, but sometimes it would be nice if you just showed it more. Let's have fun again. Lately everything feels so routine with us. Let's go out and mingle. Remember when the only place I could see you was in a crowded club? I hated that and yearned so deeply for even two hours of alone time with you, but I couldn't get it for months. Now, though, we're always alone. We work and come home. It's all about money. Let's go on a couple's retreat, or go to another country or something. I want to create new memories."

"You want to create new memories?" Her eyes lit up. "Wow."

"Yes, do you know that it's because of you that I always want to try to dance? If I'm working in a party atmosphere, I crave you and can't dance with anyone but you. I never knew how to and never liked to dance until I met you. Now every time I'm in that kind of environment it makes me miss you. The worst way to miss your partner is when you didn't even break-up, Jessie. I miss the part of you that I worked so hard to get to know. It's almost like we are going in reverse, and you're the workaholic now."

"No, I'm not," she said.

"You are too. You purposely keep yourself too busy to avoid things in your life."

"Like what?"

I paused. "Never mind. Forget I said that."

"No, what are you talking about?" She stared at me curiously.

"I'm talking about the 60-hour-work weeks, working on call, taking extra training, coming home too tired to think about..." I stopped.

A single tear rolled down her left cheek. She knew where I was going with the conversation, and I decided against saying more. I got up and walked to her side of the table. Taking her hand, I led her to the couch, and hugged her silently as she her released her long overdue tears.

A year earlier Jessie's older brother, Gabriel, was stabbed repeatedly and died in her arms. Her family, all except for her mother, blamed her for it. Gabriel had been in and out of jail for most of his adult life and was always borrowing money to finance his gambling addiction. The night he died Jessie and I were in New York visiting her family in the Bronx when he came home and asked her to borrow $600 to cover a bet. She told him no.

"Just this one last time, I promise," he pleaded.

"What is wrong with you? I said no."

Her two older sisters, who were also at home, didn't say anything, and her mother was lying down in the other room. No one knew where her father was.

Gabriel left in a huff, saying he'd find the money elsewhere or try to talk to the people he owed to hold off a few days until he could come up with it. Not too long after he walked out Jessie changed her mind, and we went to look for him at the liquor store where she knew he'd be, but it was too late. We arrived to see two men running away into the night and Gabriel bleeding and wincing in pain on the cold concrete floor in front of the store. Jessie ran to him, and I called 911, but he died coughing blood in her arms before the ambulance arrived. The news traveled fast because the whole neighborhood knew Gabriel. Her sisters ran to us as oncoming sirens wailed.

They blamed Jessie for his death because they felt if she had given him the money he would still be alive. Her mother did not fault her, however. She prayed and let it go. She said she only hoped he didn't go to hell for living badly and owing money to so many people. Six months after it happened, her mother also spoke up about how he used to steal from her and that perhaps God knew best by removing him. However, Jessie's sisters didn't feel that way and held a grudge against Jessie.

Jessie barely shed a tear at the funeral, not because it didn't hurt but because of the tension. Plus, she paid for the entire thing. After we returned to Miami, she tried to put it behind her. Jessie never discussed her brother's death. Instead, she worked longer hours, saved more money, kept busy, and pushed me away. We became two strangers, and never really released the pain until that night when I told her how I felt about our relationship.

When she finally broke down and cried, she realized like I did that she couldn't run from the issues in her life forever because they would haunt her until resolved. I told her that until she dealt with her issues she'd feel the weight of the world on her shoulders and eventually break. The good thing was that we had each other, I told her. There's nothing worse than feeling emotionally overwhelmed and not having anyone be there for you. Even though she was Ms. Strong-Independent-I-Can-Take-On-The-World-Super-Jessie to other people, I knew there was a scared little girl inside of her hiding behind that shell of a successful career.

We talked about Gabriel late into the night. She admitted to me that she did feel a little responsible, but overall she agreed with her mother. She cried, "My sisters make me feel guilty for doing good." That was one of those moments when I thought being silent would help the most, so I just let her talk and cry until she purged herself of all she'd been carrying around. We fell asleep on the couch.

Chapter 11

After our talk things were quiet. It was as if Jessie was still trying to absorb it all. She had, however, been working a bit less. Trying to rekindle the passion we once had for each other I planned a romantic evening.

I changed the blinds from white to royal blue and the light bulbs from white to red. I turned on our illusionary fireplace and placed incense and candles all over the living room and on both sides of the wall down the hallway. I prepared shrimp and lobster linguini for dinner and place a mixed CD programmed to repeat in our surround sound stereo system.

Jessie was on her way home from a massage parlor appointment that I'd set up for her. I wanted her to be relaxed from head to toe when she walked in the door. New satin sheets graced our bed, and a red rose lay on her pillow alongside a love letter. The entire house was glowing with the backdrop of soft music and crackle sound effects built into the fireplace. Sweet smelling smoke was emitted from incense sticks in red and blue bottles

Just as I started setting the table, I heard Jessie pull up. When she came in and looked around, a smile spread across her face. I went right up to her, and we embraced.

"I missed you." I whispered.

Jessie pulled me closer and hugged me tight. "What am I going to do with you?"

"I've got a few ideas," I said, pulling off my apron and chef hat.

After dinner when she went to take a steamy shower, I decided to join her. Turning her to face me, I kissed her and slid my hands up and down the curves of her body. I could feel a wetness building between my legs, so I cleared my mind of everything except Jessie. I kissed her neck and closed my eyes, becoming one with the moment. When I slid two fingers inside of her I heard the beautiful sound of her moaning my name. As I eased in and out of her, the music filled the room.

"Jessie," I whispered and softly bit her earlobe.

"Mmm, I love it."

I slid my tongue in and out of her ear, then licked her neck again as I slowly pulled my fingers out of her. Our eyes locked for a moment. Wet, hot, horny, and with a raised heartbeat, I quickly turned off the shower and stepped out. We toweled down quickly and walked naked down the candlelit hallway to the bedroom.

When Jessie saw the rose and envelope, she went to the bed. "What's this?"

"I don't know," I said smiling.

Jessie put the rose and letter on the nightstand, which also had a bowl of fruit and a washcloth on it. Then she turned off the light and climbed into bed. I paused for a moment to admire her glowing amidst the candles—her blue-gray eyes, nose, and perfect smile. Everything that I fell in love with looked brand new to me. A powerful feeling of needing and wanting her surged through me as I went to the foot of the bed. I started by kissing her feet and sucking her toes. Then I kissed my way up her calves, alternating until I reached her inner thighs.

"Mmmmm," she moaned and spread her legs.

I kissed around her center and used the tip of my tongue to give her one short, teasing lick before I moved up to her stomach and navel. My index and middle finger grazed her clit while I braced myself with my left hand.

I reached over and took a sliced orange from the bowl on my nightstand. Sensuous R & B music played as I placed one half of the orange on each of her breasts one at a time. The center of it was cut out so that the orange covered her erect nipples, and I could taste the extra sweetness when I removed the orange and sucked her breasts. Caressing one breast while licking on the other, I eagerly sucked and licked Jessie's breasts and then squeezed the remaining juice from the orange onto her stomach and licked it off. She grabbed my hair. "Sadiraaaaaaaaa."

I put the orange back and took a strawberry out of the bowl before moving back down. Using the tip of the strawberry, I traced Jessie from clit to opening a few times before giving her one long, strong lick up and down her split. Then I slid my tongue in and out.

Maxwell's soulful voice enveloped the room as Jessie wrapped her legs around my neck. I closed my eyes and was in a zone. "Till The Cops Come Knockin'" rocked the bedroom as I sped up my licks and flicked my tongue in a snake-like motion against her clit until she trembled and screamed my name. Then I moved my tongue down to taste her release.

Her moaning and screaming turned me on so much I couldn't wait to climax. She unwrapped her legs from around me and pulled me on top of her. After resting on her for a few moments, I eased out of her arms to get the strap-on to penetrate her.

"Turn around, Jess," I told her, and she did. Before putting on the strap, I kissed down her spine, her behind, her thighs, and down behind her knees and calves to the bottom of her feet. Then I kissed back up, only this time parting her cheeks and giving her a few licks and tongue insertions.

"Oh, Sadira!" she gasped and grabbed the bed.

I paused only to put on the strap-on and then asked her to rise up a little so I could enter her frontal center slowly from behind. It had been a while since I had used it and didn't want to hurt her, so I eased in as carefully as possible. When her body finally adjusted to comfortably receiving me, she responded, matching my thrusts as I sped up.

"Jessie?"

"Hm?"

"How are you feeling?"

"Good."

"Yeah? So you like it?"

"Yes, baby I do." She sounded almost out of breath. "Yes!"

"How did my tongue feel?"

"Oooohh."

I was about to reach a climax. It took all of my strength to hold out.

I withdrew the strap-on. "Turn back around for me, J." When she did, I immediately went back inside of her with the strap-on fast and hard.

"Mmmm." The pitch of her moans got higher. "Oooh."

"Jess—," I began.

"Sadira—oh, baby."

"Oh, shit."

We were both moaning. Now lying down directly on top of her, I pressed myself against her while still penetrating her, but now I was talking dirty into her ear. "You like this dick, don't you? Say you like it."

I felt her nails in my back.

"Jessie, baby, I'm about to…"

"Come on, baby."

"Oh Jessie, I'm…oh…ahh."

"Let it out, Sadira, I'm right behind you. Come on."

"Oh, oh, ahhh," I said as I climaxed. My body shook, and she came shortly after I did. A river of sweat had formed between us. I was exhausted but felt great. After I pulled out and took off the strap, I used the washcloth to wipe her body down and then my own. I placed a soft kiss on her forehead, and we fell asleep. The candles had already burned themselves out, and Lauryn Hill's "Nothing Even Matters" was playing.

Jessie's lamp woke me up. I knew she was reading the letter, but I was so tired I went back asleep

Dear Jessie,

The last few weeks between us have felt like a new beginning of some sort. We've said things that we've held on to for quite some time, and it felt good to release them. I feel like thousands of pounds have been lifted off my shoulders just from our communicating.

Jessie, you are my inner sun. You are the reason I glow and spread my happiness to anyone in my presence. People at work tease me now because I'm always grinning, and it's because of the photo of you on my desk. To tell the truth, the love I have for you exceeds mere words and ultimately defies description, but I'm trying my best to convey it here. You have no idea of the power your presence gives me.

Do you remember how we would go to the beach at night and talk until the sun came up? We would talk about everything...or you'd just listen to my jokes, laughing until your soul was cleansed. "You've got issues!" you always told me. Yeah, but you love me.

I want those smiles back.

A 20-minute conversation with you fulfilled me for days. The scent of you had me deeming every woman who wasn't you unclean. You've worked some type of alchemy on me, turning my nightmares into honey-sweet daydreams and my fears into determination. I know I may be rambling and my thoughts are coming out unorganized, but I can't write fast or long enough to let you know just how special you are to me

Jessie, just know that with every day that passes, my love for you grows inside of me. I continuously give birth to smiles and laughter. I love you and hell, if Bobby and Whitney can make it, so can we!
Love,
Sadira

Her sniffling woke me up. "Jessie, are you all right?"

She just sighed.

I sat up and took her hand, "What's wrong? Say something, Jessie."

"Nothing," she said softly.

"Then why are you crying?" The letter was next to her.

"It's just that…it's just that I feel bad after everything you've done for me, and I didn't return it to you."

"Jessie, I told you when we spoke that I should have said something earlier, but I didn't. Now that I told you, you can work on it, right?"

"Yes, I know, but it's just that I know I totally threw myself into my work after Gabriel died, practically ignoring you. Yet you stood by me. You were always there for me, but I wasn't there for you. I don't know how you put up with me. A lot of times I wondered *why* you even bothered with me."

"Jess, I stayed with you because I knew deep down you want what everyone else wants—to be loved, respected, and to be understood. Trust me, there were plenty of times that I wanted to give up on us, but that's just not me. I don't just give up because things get a little hard. I would rather literally start dating each other all over again so we don't take each other for granted. That way we'd remember why we fell in love in the first place. Then if things still did not work, *then* we should part. There is something about you that has a hold on me."

"Yeah," she said softly.

"So, that's why I bothered with you. I knew we had a special connection the moment I saw you. Ten minutes into our first real conversation I knew you felt a bond as well. I sensed it. You tried to run from it, but I chased it. I fought for you. As time passed, it was as if I *needed* you. If you would have blown me off, it would have been different, but you didn't. You were interested, yet afraid. Have I ever hurt you?"

"No, we've had disagreements and arguments, but I can't say that you really have. The feeling I have for you is hard for me to explain. It's like you're not real."

"Please, you know I'm real, and I have flaws like everyone else."

"Well, yeah, you do. You are so sensitive. A bit of weirdo you are too, leaving one bite of a hamburger in the fridge and half-full glasses of Kool-aid around the house. Sadira, we make a lot of money between the two of us. Why do you still have to drink Kool-aid?"

"Because it's one of my favorite drinks. And, anyway, I eventually eat and drink my leftovers."

"You are truly touched by something other than an angel." She smiled and shook her head.

"I know you're not talking, Ms. Baby-I'll-Cook-Some-Cereal-for-You."

"Hey, you knew that when we met. I do not cook."

"Yeah, yeah. Hey, why don't we go to Avery's tomorrow night? It's been a long time since I've been on the mic."

"Sure, you can tell them about tonight. Just kidding. Avery's sounds like fun."

"Great, come here." I pulled her closer to me and kissed her. Then we lay back down and slept until morning.

"You don't know how to call me anymore?" Khedara told me on the phone.

"I was going call you tonight."

"Liar."

"Well..."

"So, did you two talk?"

"Yes, we did, and we're seeing eye-to-eye now."

"Good, didn't I tell you?"

"Yeah, yeah, you know I'm not good at talking."

"Well shit, you're not a mute, so don't think you can write everything down. Sometimes you have to talk."

"I know. So, how are you?"

"I can't find a straight dick attached to a good-looking brother anywhere in Atlanta. Damn it now, all the good looking guys are married or gay."

I laughed. "You say it like we're out recruiting."

"Well, hell, it seems that way."

"You've got issues."

"Now you sound like Jessie," Khedara said.

"Shut it up."

"I'm just playing with you."

"Listen," I told her. "I have to go and take care of some things."

"It's Sunday."

"Praise the Lord, but I also need to get my car washed and check into some other stuff."

"What other stuff?"

"Stop meddling."

She laughed. "Okay, take care."

"Bye."

The next day I had to work late, messing up my plans to go to Avery's with Jessie and enjoy open mic, so I called her to let her know.

"Jessie, it's me. Listen, I have to work late tonight so we won't be able to go to Avery's. I was calling to see if you could pick up some dinner or something. Call me back, okay? Bye."

"Danielle," I said to my intern. "Can you bring me an Advil, please?"

"Sure."

"Thanks."

Danielle had one more week at the radio station before she went back to school. A little chubby for her height but still very attractive, she had a medium brown complexion and silky shoulder length hair. She was sweet and hardworking.

"Here you go, Sadira," she said, giving me the Advil and a cup of water. Her hand touched mine, and she looked directly into my eyes, "Is that all you want?"

"Yes, thank you."

"Sure?" she said, staring at me with her dark, snake-like eyes.

"I'm sure."

"Okay," she said and walked out.

A few minutes after she left, a guy from the mailroom came in with a small box.

"Sadira Cooper?"

"That's me." I signed his sheet.

I hesitated opening it because it had a return address I didn't recognize and no name. Inside the box was a smaller padded envelope. Assuming Jessie was probably up to something, I went ahead and opened it. A pair of panties and short note was inside: *Sadira, tonight's the night...I have a surprise for you. -Someone Special*

I sat staring at the note for a while before I picked up the phone and called Jessie again. I figured it was from her even though it wasn't her handwriting. She picked up. "Jessie, baby, where you been all day?"

"I've just been extra busy."

"You could have at least called me back."

"I didn't want to."

"Why?"

"I just didn't want to. Listen, I have a surprise for you."

I smiled. *So the note was from her.*

"Sadira, I'm going to lose my connection in this elevator. I'll call you right back, okay?"

"Elevator?"

Click.

When I turned around in my chair, I saw Danielle whom I hadn't heard come back in the room. There were only a couple people still around at that hour, and I wondered why she was still working. Before I could ask her about it, she put her hand on my shoulder.

"Surprise!" she said.

"Excuse me?" I noticed she'd closed the door behind her. "Surprise," she said again, now with both of her hands on my shoulders as if she were about to give me a massage.

"Danielle, hold on. What are you doing? You can't just touch me."

"Shh, I heard your girl isn't fulfilling you." She began massaging my shoulders. I noticed she smelled like Jessie when she leaned down and kissed me on my earlobe. . I almost lost myself within her scent and the softness of her touch until the door opened and Jessie walked in. *Oh, shit!*

"Hey, Sadira, I'm sorry about the elev—" She stopped in her tracks when she saw Danielle's hands on me. Her mouth opened, and I saw pain in her eyes.

Everything was happening so fast. I remembered the phone calls. As she approached with an angry look, I said, "Jessie, please wait, wait, wait!" I quickly jumped up out of my chair, but it was too late. She grabbed Danielle by her hair and pulled her toward the door.

"So *this* is the bitch!" she yelled. "Oh hell no, she didn't put her hands on my—"

"Jessie, hold on!" I shouted.

"Sadira, we're getting ready to start the next seg—"

The DJ, Kevin burst into the room. He stopped talking when he saw all the drama.

Jessie was now staring daggers at me. "Sadira, you fucking bitch! How could you?"

"But, baby, I didn't…"

Danielle went over to Jessie while Jessie was fussing at me. She hit her and yelled, "Bitch, if you knew how to satisfy your woman, I wouldn't be here." She was breathing hard.

"Popcorn, *please,*" The guy from the mailroom said. "There's nothing more entertaining than a catfight!"

Where the hell did he come from? I wondered.

Jessie turned on Danielle, "I know this little Miami-Dade-Community-College trick didn't just fix her mouth to call me a bitch. Little girl, I will slap those twisted teeth out of your mouth, okay!"

"I go to Florida Memorial!"

"Stop, Jessie!" I said grabbing her. *Twisted teeth?* Did she just say twisted teeth? That shit was funny as hell, but I couldn't laugh. She would have truly hurt Danielle had I not stopped her. Suddenly in all the commotion, my boss, Mr. Carson appeared.

I let go of Jessie and tried to pull myself together.

"What is going on in here?" he asked.

The room was silent. Jessie looked at me, down at the floor, and up again at me. Tears were cascading from her eyes. She sniffed and said softly, "Goodbye, Sadira," then walked out. My first instinct was to run after her, and I did start toward the door, but I felt my boss' hand on my shoulder.

"Sadira," he said in his deep voice.

"Mr. Carson, please, I promise. I just need five minutes." I went toward the door to follow Jessie.

"Sadira!" he said. "I'm severely understaffed, so if you walk out that door, it's final."

"Final?" I was shocked that he would take it there.

"Final," he said firmly and glared at me.

"Please?"

"I don't have time, Sadira."

Hot tears were building up in my eyes. I noticed a bag on the floor that Jessie had dropped when she first walked in. Danielle was standing next to Mr. Carson. *She's probably fucking him too*, I thought. There was dead silence.

"I'll be back for my things," I told him.

He looked surprised. "You're leaving?"

"Mr. Carson, my life just walked out the door. Yes, I'm leaving."

"Well then pack up and go right now."

"Now?"

"Is there a comprehension problem? Yes, now."

I wanted to choke Danielle, but I restrained myself. I just lost my girl and my job, and I couldn't think straight. I picked up a cardboard box from the corner and threw all of my personal belongings in it. I was in too much pain to be embarrassed.

"Mr. Carson, why don't you let her come back?" said Kevin.

"Kevin, do you like your job here?"

"Uh…yeah."

"Then I suggest you stick to playing music and not meddling."

Steve, who was one of the building security guards arrived to escort me out. Without looking at him, I put the bag that Jessie left in the box with my things and carried them out with my head hanging down and tears falling.

"I'm sorry," Steve said to me when we got to the exit. Steve and I had become casual friends. He was a dark skin brother. No, Steve was black like under-the-kitchen-sink-at-night black, but his skin was silk smooth and he was well built. At the moment, I don't think he knew what else to say. Nor did I.

"Call me if you need to, Sadira," he told me.

"Yeah, thanks," I said softly with a sniffle.

I walked straight to my car and put the box in the trunk. I couldn't push myself too hard, or I'd have chest pains or an asthma attack. It was only at tense times like this that my heart murmur or asthma acted up, and the last thing I needed was to be in physical distress.

By the time I got home I was drained. *This has got to be a dream.* But it wasn't. Jessie didn't even look at me, much less speak. As a matter of fact, she went into our bedroom and slammed the door. Then she locked it. I didn't know what to do. I felt tired and a little dizzy too. Then I remembered I hadn't taken my medication all day.

I knocked on the door and begged her to open it, but it was to no avail. I did the only thing I knew how to do. I got down on my knees and prayed. I lost track of how long I prayed, but when I got up the house was deathly silent. I knocked on the door again, but I heard nothing.

"Jessie? Jessie, please just talk to me."

No answer. She didn't even acknowledge my presence.

"Jess," I said softly and eased back down to the floor at the door. "Jessie," I said again and knocked on the door. "Jessie, I need my pills."

A moment later she unlocked the door, opened it a crack, and threw an orange medication bottle at me.

"Not these!" I yelled. I tried to push the door open before she locked it again, but I was not quick enough.

Jessie slammed the door, barely missing my fingers.

"That's all you have in here, Sadira," she said from the other side of the door. She finally spoke, but those were not the words I wanted to hear.

"Jessie, that's not all, I need my other pills. I don't feel well."

"You don't have anything else in here."

I went to the hallway bathroom to check, but they weren't there either. *Where the hell were my pills?* I checked my pockets again. Then I searched the kitchen and the living room, but I didn't find them. I went back out to my car and rummaged through the glove compartment, then the box with my stuff from the job. *My job!* I reached in my pocket for my cell phone and called the station. I got the security desk.

"Steve?"

"Hold on," someone said.

"Hello?" It was Steve's voice.

"Steve, it's Sadira."

"Hey, you dropped a bottle of pills."

"My medication? You have it?"

"Yes, it's right here."

"All right, I'm coming to get it right now."

"Okay."

"See you soon." I hung up and jumped in the car.

It was a hard drive. I was so tired. When I pulled up in front of the radio station, the parking lot was almost empty except for a couple of cars. Quickly, I went inside to meet Steve.

"Hey, Sadira. I tried to call your cell phone after you left, but I got a fast busy signal." He handed me the bottle of pills.

"Oh, I don't know what happened, but thanks anyway."

"You don't look so good. Let me get you some water." He headed off to the cooler.

I opened the bottle and took two pills out. When he returned, I took them with a swallow of water from the cup he brought. I told him, "I'm not feeling well."

"What's wrong?" I heard someone ask. I turned to see that it was Danielle, and a wave of anger surged through me.

"Are you crazy?" I yelled at her. "What are you talking to me for?" I lunged at her, but Steve grabbed me.

"I was just…" she said weakly.

"I wonder how you ever got into college because you are *not* the sharpest fucking pencil. Now back the fuck up!"

Steve had me in a grip of death, so I couldn't move.

"Leave," he told to her. "Leave!"

When she turned to go, I broke down and sobbed. I buried my face in Steve's chest. My burst of energy was gone, and now I felt only pain. As Danielle walked way, Steve's hold turned into a consoling hug.

"Don't worry," he said, "things are going to work out for you. Jessie just needs time to cool down, that's all."

I couldn't talk. All I could do was cry. I'd worked so hard to patch things up at home, and in an instant it all crumbled, taking my job with it. Now I had to go back home.

As I turned to leave, Steve said, "Sadira, why don't you call someone to pick you up? I don't think you should drive."

"I don't have anyone else," I said, wiping tears from my face.

"Not even Jessie?"

"No, she won't even talk to me."

"Well, stay here with me until you get yourself together."

"I'll be okay."

"No, I think you should hang around until you feel better."

"I'll be fine. I just need to go to the bathroom and fix myself up."

"Okay," he sighed.

When I went in to the bathroom, I could hear the music down the hall from the midnight love segment. I didn't even want to be in the station, but I felt I needed something to make me more alert. I splashed cold water on my face and popped another two pills. *Oh shit, why did I do that?* I reprimanded myself before trying to throw them back up, but I couldn't. I had already taken two when Steve brought me water from the cooler. Then I heard sniffling from one of the stalls.

"Are you all right in there?" No answer. "Hello? Are you all right in there?" I asked again. The door opened, and it was Danielle. "Damn, I can't get rid of you."

She looked hurt. "I'm sorry, Sadira. I really am sorry."

"Yeah, well, you should be! What the hell is wrong with you? What were you thinking?"

"I was thinking that I know how you feel."

I sighed. "I don't know why I'm even talking to you. Goodbye."

"Because you're in pain, and as usual Jessie isn't here for you, that's why."

"What are you saying, girl?" My mind told me to leave, but my heart told me to stay and listen.

"I'm saying I know you've been hurting on the inside because I see a reflection of myself in you."

I remained silent.

"I don't know all the facts, but I'm assuming Jessie is leaving a void in you. She's so wrapped up in herself that she doesn't see the good in you."

"Don't talk about her like that." I was fatigued and felt nauseous.

"You know it's true."

I ignored her and walked toward the door, but she stepped in front of me.

"All you want is to be noticed, to be appreciated, to have your back rubbed after a long day, to have someone who loves you back the way you love them."

I wanted to avoid what she was saying, but she was directly in front of me. I didn't have enough energy to fight with her either.

"What you need is someone who values you."

"Move, Danielle," I told her, but she didn't. She was so close that you probably couldn't slide a sheet of paper between us. I could literally feel her breath.

"She left you crying and hurt. You shouldn't be crying. You're a good woman. You need someone like me who can give you what you deserve." She leaned forward and kissed me on my cheek.

"Move out of my way." *Damn, I'm tired.*

"Sadira," she whispered in my ear. "I won't do you like she did." When Danielle tried to kiss my lips, I snapped out of the trance she was putting me in and backed up.

No, this is wrong, I thought.

"She probably already assumed we slept together anyway," she said, leaning closer. "I won't treat you the way she does." Her tongue grazed my bottom lip.

"No! I can't do this. Jessie is still my girl. No! This is wrong and it's all your fucking fault, so move!" I pushed her aside and walked out.

I waved goodbye to Steve and left the building. When I got in my car, the first thing I did was call Khedara, but she didn't answer her home or cell. Because I felt so physically drained, I made sure to put on my seat belt before heading home on I-95. Soon my chest tightened and my breathing became labored. I slowed down and reached in my glove compartment for my inhaler, hoping it would help.

My phone rang. The caller ID said it was my sister.

"Hey, Khedara."

"Hey, girl, what's up?"

"Sis, my whole life is falling apart." I wiped my sweaty hands on my pants.

"What?"

"I'll tell you all about it when I get home, but Jessie and I had a huge fight. I can't even get into my own bedroom *and* I lost my job."

"What the hell happened?"

"Too much, but I'm tired right now so just stay on the phone with me. As a matter of fact, hold on, let me use my earpiece instead."

My hands started shaking, my vision blurred, and I heard a loud horn blow. "Sadira!" was the last thing I heard from my sister. The phone fell from my hands as my car spun out of control. I felt hard thumps all around me. Shattered windshield glass pierced my skin. The airbag came out, and I heard the pounding of my own heartbeat before everything went coal black.

Chapter 12

Next I felt a burning and stinging sensation rush through my body, which was trapped inside the car. My God, it hurt. I wanted to scream but was unable to. I couldn't see anything but the darkness of night, and the octopus of death was slowly wrapping its arms around me. *I can't breathe,* I thought, feeling the life being squeezed out of me. Every moment seemed fatal as I struggled to remain conscious. The car was on its side, I think, and I was pinned against the driver's side door. I still couldn't see anything. Everything looked black, and I was relying on all my other senses.

Thoughts and questions stampeded through my mind. *Where is my inhaler? My legs are stinging!* "Jessie, " was all I could get out. *I need my inhaler.* Feeling around for it, I touched glass and liquid. *Liquid? Was I bleeding or was that old Kool-aid? Where was my pump? I just had it in my lap!* My eyelids felt heavy, so I closed them. The sound of my heartbeat grew louder to the point that I thought it was going to burst, and my life was measured in slow, loud heartbeats. I tried my best to suck air in, but my lungs wouldn't cooperate.

The sound of an ambulance screamed in the distance. I had an agonizing headache. When my phone rang, I felt around for it but instead found my inhaler. *I found it!* It was a struggle to get it to my mouth, but I managed to get one good pull. I felt my lungs instantly open up.

"Hold on, just hold on," I heard a man say.

My phone was still ringing, but I couldn't get to it.

"Hello?" I heard the man's voice say.

Did he just answer my phone? As the ambulance got closer, the sirens were replaced by the gallop of my heartbeat. I now heard many voices around me. My vision was back, but it was useless since everything I saw was a fuzzy yellowish blur.

"Does she drive a blue Benz?" I heard the man say. "Well, you need to get down here quick, she's had a really bad accident. She's at the Pembroke Pines exit off I-95. "

Shit, I'm less than five minutes from home!

"Hang on in there, honey!" a woman said. "We're going to need the Jaws of Life to get her out."

The Jaws of Life? "Call Jessie… " I said.

"Shh, don't try to talk," the woman said.

It seemed like an eternity before I heard a familiar voice, "Sadira, oh my God!"

"Ms., I'm going to need you to back up," someone said.

"Sadira!"

"Ms., please stand back."

"No, YOU back up!"

Jessie was there. The stinging sensation faded, but my body felt numb. I heard a loud chatter of voices. It was chaos.

"Is she allergic to… " I thought I heard.

"No," Jessie said, sounding agitated. "She has asthma, a heart murmur, and sickle cell anemia. What hospital are you going to?" I could hear her was crying.

"Jackson Memorial," a paramedic answered.

"God, I felt it. I had bad feeling in the pit of my stomach." Jessie cried hysterically.

"Ms., I'm going to need you to stand back," a medic said.

Rescue workers hurried toward me with a machine that seemed to have claw-like arms. I guessed it was the Jaws of Life. The sound was deafening, one I'll never forget. They used it quickly to cut the roof of the car and pull me out.

People were everywhere—taking my blood pressure, my pulse. They put me on a stretcher and wrapped my legs after putting an oxygen mask over my mouth. I felt faint again so I closed my eyes and tried to settle myself. Then I blacked out.

The next time I woke up I was on a hard hospital bed. To my left was Khedara, to my right was Jessie, and at the foot of the bed was Steve. The room was bright white, except for the flowers.

"What happened?" I asked.

Jessie took a deep breath and looked at my sister before speaking, "Well, you've been asleep off and on since last night. You had a car accident. You spun out of control, hit a pole, four trees on each side of the car and stopped just short of a canal. I'm so sorry," she said in tears.

The eyes of Jessie and Khedara looked red from crying while dry-eyed Steve had a grim, worried look on his face. It wasn't until a doctor walked in with a chart that I really looked around. I was hooked up to two machines and couldn't feel my left leg.

"Do they have any red Kool-Aid in here?" I asked softly.

Steve laughed. "After all you been through, Sadira, Kool-Aid is what you ask for?"

Jessie shook her head, "She hasn't changed. And how many times do I have to tell you that red is the color, not the flavor." She smiled at me affectionately

"Whatever," I said.

"They don't have any damn Kool-Aid, Sadira," Khedara said and grinned.

"Why y'all acting like you don't drink Kool-Aid?" I laughed, but my chuckle quickly turned into a coughing spell. A nurse brought me water.

"May I have some packets of sugar to go with this water, please?" I asked her.

"No, Ms. Cooper, I'm sorry I can't do that." The nurse shook her head and smiled.

The doctor came in and said, "She needs to get some rest." Moments later when everyone left, the doctor explained the situation to me.

I suffered from internal bleeding. He said my nervous system had shut down, but it was now coming back up. I was so tired that his words melted into each other and I only caught certain parts of what he was saying. I may or may not be able to walk again, he told me, and the tree that hit the driver's side had smashed the door into my leg.

Suddenly I understood the magnitude of what happened. "No, no, no!" I cried. "Hell no, this can't be for real." My seatbelt plus the airbag coming out is what saved me from going through the windshield into the canal. I told the doctor I was tired, and he left.

"No, I don't want it! No life support!"

"Sadira," a tearful Jessie pleaded.

"No! Living by life support is not living."

Khedara, not normally one to cry, was in tears.

"Ouch!"

"What?" they both asked.

"Pain," I said and began coughing. After my coughing spell I blacked out.

"Sadira, Sadira, wake up!" I heard Jessie's frantic voice. In a cold sweat I swallowed hard and looked around. A dream, that's what this was. I was having a bad dream. I felt a powerful throbbing in my left leg off and on without warning. Jessie's face was flushed with hurting as she took my hand and locked my fingers in hers. Khedara was crying. Obviously, she felt my pain and the frustration of being powerless to help me.

"I'll be right back, I'm going to the bathroom," Jessie said and kissed my forehead.

The good news turned out to be that I wasn't as bad as the doctors originally thought and I would be released and in physical therapy within another week or so.

I wondered why did this all have to happen to me? Why couldn't things just work out happily for me? Why am I the way I am? Why are there more people afraid of a broken heart than there are people afraid of dying? Why had my life turned into such a downward spin of heartache? Why did bad things keep happening to me? I felt like I was drowning in a grainy pool of pain. Would there be no happiness in this life for me?

As I was in the midst of my endless questioning of life, the door opened and in walked Danielle. I pushed the button for the nurse.

"Get out of here!" I yelled at her and pushed the button again.

"Oh my God, I heard what happened," she said. "Sadira, I'm sorry."

"Nurse!" I yelled, repeatedly while pushing the button. "Nurse, nurse! Jesus, I can't take this."

Just then Jessie and Khedara came in. "Who is this?" asked my sister.

"You must want me to beat you down again," said Jessie, looking directly at Danielle statue-still and ready to fight.

"*This* is Danielle?" Khedara asked.

"I just came to see how she was doing," Danielle said.

"I've got news for you, trifling bitch!" shouted Jessie. "Because of you, Sadira almost died. Get the fuck out. You are not welcome here! I swear to God you have two seconds before I put your ass in intensive care. You scandalous, dirty cunt!"

The nurse rushed in with a concerned look. "Is everything okay?"

"No," I said. "Leave. I want everyone out of my room. I'm tired," I said, surprising myself. I wanted to be totally alone. Jessie looked at me with tears in her eyes. I could see the hurt deep inside of her, but at the moment I needed peace and quiet. She left, and I drifted off to sleep.

"Sadira?" I heard. "Sadira?"

I opened my eyes and saw Jessie.

"Sadira," she said again and kissed me on the forehead.

"Hey, Jess," I said. I felt calmer now

"How are you feeling?"

I sighed. "Give me your hand," I told her and she did. "Close your eyes, I want to pray."

"Okay."

"God, I'm struggling with my faith right now. Jessie and I are going through strong trials. I'm asking You right now that no matter what we face, please help us to hang on to our belief in You and in our own integrity. God, I'm asking that You give us both the strength to work through this and the vision to see Your hand in all of it. In Your son's name we pray. Amen." When I looked at Jessie, she was blinking back tears.

"Jessie," I said.

"Yes?"

"I didn't do anything with her. I've never cheated on you and have no intention to. I know what it looked like, but nothing happened."

Jessie didn't say anything. She just listened.

"I want you to know…"

But before I could finish talking, Khedara walked in and not too long after that Steve and the DJ, Kevin, arrived with flowers and get-well balloons. I smiled.

Chapter 13

As the days passed, I made progress and needed less pain medication. When I was finally released from the hospital, I was immediately placed in a physical therapy program at a facility in Ft. Lauderdale. Before I knew it a month had gone by and autumn arrived, casting a yellow, heat-filled haze over the city.

Jessie helped me into her Rav4 after picking me up from my therapy session. I had another week and a half to go, and then I'd be finished. At first, it had been terribly difficult for me. I almost ended up back in the hospital after I fell down. I had tried to walk without my crutches too soon. Humbled, I relied on Jessie to get me around because my car was totally wrecked between the accident and the Jaws of Life cutting it open.

"How are you feeling?" Jessie asked.

"I'm hungry. Can we stop at Checkers and get a chicken sandwich or something?"

"All right."

Jessie took me to get something to eat, then dropped me off at home before leaving to go back to work.

"If you need anything call me," she said on her way out.

"I'll be fine. See you later."

"Okay, miss me," she said with a smile.

"I will. Bye."

I planted myself on the couch and watched videos and old South Park episodes until she came back later that evening.

After giving me a bath and helping me into my pajamas, she said, "Sadira?"

"Yeah, sweetie?"

She paused. "Never mind."

"What's up?"

"It's just…" she began and paused. "It's just that sometimes I wonder what would have happened if I didn't walk in on you and Danielle when I did."

"Nothing would have happened." I said as I eased into bed. "Nothing, do you hear me?"

"How can you be so sure? She was giving you a massage, a package with panties were on your desk, plus she had on a short ass, come-fuck-me skirt."

"I just said…"

"You always said how helpful your intern was and how well she followed your instructions and—"

"Jessie, that was about work. I didn't know anything about her ulterior motives."

"And she even called our house! I wish I would see her ass in the streets again. The bitch called our fucking house, blatantly disrespecting me."

"I'm sorry." We were quiet for a few minutes. Looking directly into her eyes, I said "Jessie, listen to me, I've never looked at Danielle as more than an intern. I had no intentions of sleeping with her or with anyone else besides you."

She was silent.

I said, "Now, I know things haven't really been smooth since our last talk, but think about it. Why would I go through the trouble of communicating my feelings with you to strengthen our relationship just to go cheat on you and mess it all up? Think about it, Jessie. C'mon now, sweetie it just doesn't make sense."

She lowered her head and spoke softly. "This wouldn't have happened if I would have satisfied you in the first place."

I remembered Danielle said the same thing, but I wasn't about to say so. Jessie kept her eyes focused on her lap, then sighed.

"Let's go to sleep," I said. "Let it go."

"All right, I'll let it go. I'm going to take a quick shower. I'll be back."

I turned off the lights.

It was almost 2:00 in the morning when I woke up from a restless sleep. As quietly as I could without waking Jessie, I got my crutches and went into our home office. I wanted to write a couple of poems and start working on a photo-essay book that had been on my mind for the last couple of months. Getting around was becoming a little easier for me, and I couldn't wait to be rid of the crutches entirely. As the computer started, I softly played one of my Hidden Beach jazz CD's. The instrumental version of Will Smith's "Summertime" floated through the room. It was so low you could barely hear it, but it was enough music to get me going.

Later I yawned as the sun came up. Just when I placed my head on the desk like a schoolgirl sleeping in class, Jessie opened the door with sleep written all over her face.

"Hey, how long have you been in here?"

"Half of the night. I'm tired now."

"Do you want to lay back down, or do you want me to make you some cereal or something?"

I grinned.

"Don't start with the cooking jokes," she said but laughed anyway.

It had been awhile since we shared a smile like that. "I'm actually going to go back and lie down. You go on and get ready for work. One of us has to keep a job."

"All right. Don't hesitate to call if you need me."

"I won't."

I spent the rest of the day and week for that matter, lounging around and ordering things from the home shopping network. One day Jessie came home and found me sitting in the middle of opened boxes and peanuts, popping the bubble wrap that came with the things I bought. I'd ordered all kinds of things that I absolutely had no use for, and they all seemed to arrive at the same time.

"You better put that shit up for sale on Ebay," she said laughing. "Damn, we have to get you a job before you become addicted to shopping."

"I'm going to get a job as soon as I can walk on my own, trust me. I want to get back to work."

She was very gentle and caring during my recovery. I couldn't remember the last time I sat around just doing nothing. The following week I wrote a couple of poems and organized my photo collection.

"Hey, Jessie, check this out," I said to her one day.

"What's up?"

I dramatically dropped my crutches down one at a time and walked to her. Her face lit up and a smile spread across it.

"Oh, look at you!" she said, clapping her hands.

"Watch me strut, girl," I said and laughed.

"You've still got issues."

When I turned the radio on, Jay-Z and Pharell's "Frontin'" was playing. "Uh oh, you know that's our song."

"Silly," she said and laughed at me dancing by myself. It felt great to be back on my feet.

I was able to get a new car after my insurance company sorted everything out. I got the same type of Benz I had before the accident, but a black one this time. I really wanted to find a job though. Things seemed to slow down after my physical therapy, and I got depressed sometimes when I was at home alone while Jessie worked. I tried my best to hold on to my faith and respect the necessary pain in changing and being pulled out of my comfort zone. I really liked my old job, but there was no way I'd go back, not even if Mr. Carson himself called me. I thought about Devonte and JD up at the station in New York. *Tricia,* I remembered, but quickly put her out of my mind.

One quiet Sunday when Jessie was working at home and I toyed around with my photography portfolio, I realized I felt lonely. I wondered why I felt lonely when Jessie was only a few feet away from me. *What was wrong with me?*

Chapter 14

The next days, weeks, and months passed quickly. It was the holiday season again, and my usual loneliness came back. I tried to fill the emptiness by hanging out at Avery's. I read a poem every now and then there, and the environment at Avery's kept me from falling deeper into depression. My relationship with Jessie felt like it had rewound all the way back to the beginning, and I was unhappy all over again. I still didn't have a full-time job, but I had a temporary one through an agency at a small radio station. Actually it was a temp-to-perm assignment, but I had a good feeling about it. My problem was with Jessie and me, which was causing the emptiness I was feeling.

The car accident had stripped me of my old self. I was broken down and put back together. It felt like my heart was floating in a shoreless ocean of fierce desolation. Something was missing from my soul. I realized that Jessie and I would sink into a deadening routine if things didn't change soon. I didn't even know what we could change that we had not tried before.

One day I went into the bathroom, got down on my knees and prayed for guidance. It was all I knew how to do. I was truly afraid of what would become of us. All I wanted was to have someone who cared for me the way that I cared for them. I loved Jessie wholeheartedly. I think I loved her more than I loved myself, but I didn't think I could allow myself to feel that way anymore.

"What's wrong, Sadira?" Jessie asked at dinner that night.
"Nothing."

"So why have you been so quiet and distant lately?"

"I don't know."

"What's with the short answers? What's going on?"

"I don't know, okay?" I snapped. "I'm going to do some work." I got up from the table and went in our office. I didn't quite know how to say that was I was starting to feel resentment and anger toward her again especially since the next Saturday was the anniversary of us becoming a couple.

"Sadira," she said, following me.

I felt her hands on my shoulders. "Yes?"

"What's wrong, baby girl?"

"I guess I'm a little annoyed."

"About what?"

I sighed. "Things are back to the way they used to be with us, Jessie."

"I thought we were getting better."

"We were for awhile, but…. I don't know. Oh, never mind, I'll be fine."

"I want to show you something," she said. "I'll be right back."

"Okay." I stood in the hall, staring out of the window. A woman walking down the block caught my attention. She had a beautiful brown complexion that glowed in the sun. I'd never seen her in the neighborhood before, but a few seconds later Jessie returned and I turned my attention back to her.

She handed me three journals. "Take a look at these," she said.

"What are they?"

"They're all the things I should have said to you verbally."

"Huh?"

"Every time you made me feel special, I wrote it down. I also wrote down the fear that followed my initial happiness. I know it's a lot, but I'd planned on giving you this months ago."

"Wow. How long have you been writing this stuff?"

"Since we moved to Miami."

"Jesus, since we moved? How much more are you holding on to? I'm getting sick of you rationing out your goddamned feelings, Jessie. I can't believe with all the shit we've gone through that you still kept this type stuff all to yourself."

"Yes," she said softly, "it's like in the back of my mind I was just waiting for you to mess up. But you never did. I was still afraid to totally let go, though I see now…I see a look in your eyes that I've never seen before, and I don't know what it is. Don't give up on me, please."

I didn't know what to say.

"Just read through them," she said, looking at me with pleading eyes.

Although her words were a little overwhelming, I continued reading her journals all night.

One day you're going to hurt me, but I hope not. I'm in love with you, Sadira. Please don't let me down. I'm in too deep right now to turn back. I want to be the girl of your dreams, but I don't know how. Why do I feel like a stranger to you? Never mind, it's because I never honestly revealed the core of myself to you.

The sun came up differently today, and I think I've fallen even deeper in love with you. You mean so much to me, and I feel as though every time I write it in here instead of telling you I'm stunting our relationship by protecting myself. This is the best I can do for now, but one day I'll show you. I'm so proud of you for all the things you've got going on. You're a trailblazer and an inspiration. I don't know how you do all that you do with only 24 hours in the day, but I'm proud of you. You've touched so many people with your sense of humor, your photography, your poetry, your—I could go on and on. I do love you. You mean a lot to me, and I'm glad we met that day on the train. You keep me on track spiritually.

There was much more, and I kept reading until I felt numb. I was in awe of how much Jessie still held on to her feelings when all I asked her to do was to express them. I didn't even know what I would say to her when I finally crept into bed. She was asleep. Lying on my back, I looked up and mouthed thank you to God before I turned on my side and pulled her close to me. I kissed her on the back of her neck, and she arched into me. I soon closed my eyes and drifted off to sleep beside her.

The next morning was awkward. I still didn't quite know what to say to Jessie, but I knew I had to say something. I wasn't even sure of how I felt. A part of me was happy to have been exposed to her feelings, but another part of me was bitter knowing that she held the key to our relationship getting better. How could she be so selfish? Were there not two hearts involved, hers *and* mine?

"Hey," she said when she came out of the bathroom.

"Good morning." I was still in bed, but I planned on getting up soon. I wasn't working that day. I wanted to go out and take new photographs.

"So?" she said expectantly.

"It was deep." That was all I could say.

"That's it?"

"Well, I'm still trying to absorb it all. It was a lot."

"Oh." Looking disappointed, she continued getting dressed.

"Thanks for sharing though," I said, but it didn't come out the way I wanted it to. My tone was rather dry and unaffectionate. I was uncomfortable, and I wanted her to leave so I could gather my thoughts.

"Hey, do you want to meet me for lunch today?" she asked.

"What?"

"You heard me."

"Oh, I mean you just caught me in mid-thought. Sure, what time?"

"About 1:00, but I'll call you to make sure the time doesn't change,"

"Sure," I said.

Fifteen minutes later she was gone, and by 9:30 I was up and out of the house.

While I was out shooting, I photographed mainly elderly people and women with children, as well as a few shots of the clouds in the sky. At 12:45 Jessie called to move lunch to 1:30. That was fine with me. I could sort out my feelings while I shot pictures. Reading Jessie's journals made me feel like a kid who asked for the same toy over and over, but never got it until after she didn't want it anymore, or forgot why she wanted it in the first place. It was a feeling of being so aggravated by the time I got it that I barely enjoyed or wanted it.

At 1:00 I stopped my shooting and got in my car. I drove to Pollo Tropical where we had a simple lunch. It was cool to meet up in the middle of the day. We hadn't done it in ages.

"How's your day so far? asked Jessie.

"Enlightening. And yours?"

"Hectic, but in a good way."

"Well, that's good."

Our lunch date ended up being devoid of serious conversation. We finished eating and hugged goodbye.

"Oh, Sadira, don't forget to pick up your prescriptions from the pharmacy," she said after starting her jeep.

"I won't. See you later."

"Bye sweetie," was the last thing she said before driving off.

Chapter 15

I stopped at Walgreens to pick up my medication and was opening my door when I noticed a woman with a light brown complexion and a natural ethnic hairstyle getting out of the car next to mine. She was dressed in winter white pants and a buttercup yellow turtleneck covered by a lab coat. It was the same woman I saw through the window the day Jessie gave me the journals.

I wanted to say something, but I felt weird. Damn, she was even prettier up close. *I should say something*, I told myself, but I couldn't. Jessie would kill me, especially since she just revealed to me how she always knew in the back of her mind I would mess up and hurt her. *Fuck,* I thought.

"Excuse me?" I ended up saying to my own surprise. *Uh oh, no, no, no, you shouldn't be approaching her,* I told myself.

"Yes?" she said. Oh my God, she had such striking green eyes! Contacts or not, they looked terrific on her and certainly matched her electrifying appeal. She looked somehow familiar to me though I know I'd never spoken to her before.

I swallowed hard and took a deep breath. "Well, um, I'm a photographer and wanted to know if you'd be interested in being the subject of one of my shoots." I immediately wondered if I said the right thing, but it was too late to take my words back. I sensed I was about to be rejected.

"What kind of shoot?"

My mouth opened in surprise that she wasn't brushing me off. "It's sort of like, you know…"

She laughed. "What do you really want from me?"

"The real deal is I think you're attractive, and since I probably won't get to see you again, I thought that if I photographed you, I could at least hold on to your still image." I surprised myself with my boldness and was pleased that I said what I had to say.

She studied me and jingled her keys as if it would help her decide what to do. "When?"

"Excuse me?"

"When do you want to do this and where?" she said, with a touch of flirtatiousness.

"How about at a park sometime during the day?"

"Okay, I see. Well, I wouldn't mind. Are you going to give me your phone number, or should I wait until we meet at Walgreens again?"

"Aren't you funny," I said smiling. "Sure, I'll give you my number. Wait, I mean No! I mean…I live with my girlfriend, and I can't."

"Girlfriend?"

"Yes, I have a girl. That's why I said I probably won't get to see you again."

"Well, thank you for your honesty, but if you have a girlfriend, then why do you want a picture of me?"

I hesitated. "We're just going through some things right now, but in all honesty. I really am working on a photo collection."

"Okay. Well, then, let me give you my number." She reached in her purse for a card. I don't want to call your place and get you in trouble."

I still couldn't believe what I was doing or how I would act around Jessie when I got home. In all the time we'd been together, I never approached another woman—well, besides—Tricia but she didn't count. Jessie and I weren't officially a couple at that time.

"Thanks," I said after she gave me her card. "I have to get home now."

"And I have shopping to do. I'm still settling in, but that's another conversation."

"All right. Hey?"

"Yeah?"

"Never mind." I decided not to ask if she was the woman I'd seen on my block.

"Okay, talk to you later, um…"

"Sadira! That's my name." I looked down at the piece of paper she gave me. "Nice meeting you, Kenya."

She smiled and nodded, and we went our separate ways.

"Khedara." I called her as soon as I got home since. Jessie hadn't arrived yet.

"Hey, girl, what's up? How are you feeling?"

"I'm pretty good, and I didn't even have to get addicted to painkillers."

She laughed. "So what's up?"

"I met someone today."

"You what?"

I cleared my throat. "I met someone and took her phone number."

"Sadira, are you nuts? What did you go and do that for?"

"I don't know. I wasn't out looking, but we just kind of met."

"So why'd you take her number?"

"Why not?"

"The name Jessie comes to mind."

"Well, I told her that I have a girlfriend and only took the number to set up a photo shoot."

"So you're going to see her again?"

"Yes, but not alone. In a park, out in the open, in public."

"Mm hm."

"What?"

"You're attracted to her."

"Yes, I am. I have to admit it. I don't know why all of this is happening. No, I mean, I do. I'm not satisfied at home, and ever since the car accident it's gotten worse. Even though she took good care of me, I still felt emptiness. I'm starting to see things in a new light, and Jessie has slipped back into the way she used to be. She did share her journals with me, but they didn't have the impact either of us thought they would. They weren't enough to stop me from taking someone else's number."

"Her journals?"

"Yep, all of this time. Whenever I made her feel any kind of way, especially good, she wrote it down instead of telling me. She had three journals full of feelings that she kept from me."

"Wow, that's deep. What are you going to do?"

"That's what I called you for."

"I don't know what to tell you."

"C'mon, Khedara, you have to know."

She was quiet.

"Help me out, I'm confused. I don't want to hurt Jessie, but I've been silently hurting inside for a long time."

"The only thing I can suggest you do is have another sit-down with her and if things still don't change, take some time apart."

Her words hit me hard. I couldn't believe we had really reached that point. I hadn't been in a bed without Jessie in so long. It hurt just to think about it. Our anniversary was coming up.

"Are you there?" asked Khedara

"Yeah," I said as I heard Jessie pulling into the driveway. "Well, she's here now. I'll call you back later."

"Okay," she said and hung up.

Jessie walked in carrying a box of pizza. "Hey, sweetie."

"Hey, you," I said, taking the box from her.

She put her bag down and went straight to the kitchen. "What are you up to?"

"Nothing much. I'm about to watch The Color Purple though."

She laughed. "Why?"

"Because I haven't seen it in a while. Are you going to keep quizzing me or sit down and watch Sofia and Harpo?"

She shook her head laughing. "Something is wrong with you, I know it."

"What?"

"Nothing," she said smiling.

"Well, sit down if you want to watch the movie because I'm about to rewind it for you."

"Okay, okay."

By the end of the movie she was snuggled in my arms. We were full from the pizza and Pepsi, but it was still early. After Jessie and I cleaned up the living room and kitchen together, I asked her, "Hey, do you want to go to the beach?"

"On a Wednesday night?"

"Sure, it's only 8:00. We can go to Hallandale."

"I would, baby girl, but I'm tired."

"Okay." I heard the disappointment in my own voice.

She sighed. "You really want to go to the beach, don't you?"

"Yes, but never mind."

"But it's cold out…" She paused, then said, "Fine," and smiled. "We can go."

"For real?"

"Yes."

"Great," I said and grinned. I was happy. "And it's not all that cold. Come on, New Yorker, this Miami winter should be easy for you."

As Jessie drove across Miramar Parkway toward Hallandale Beach, I put in an R. Kelly mixed CD, and "Raindrops" was the first song to play. The ride was quiet except for the music. I occasionally glanced over at her as she drove.

The beach was almost empty at that hour. There were only a few couples out, and it was a peaceful night under the south Florida sky. A full moon was shining. I took her hand, and we walked barefoot along the shore. We stopped every now and then to stare off into the water and embrace. It felt good to be with Jessie like that, but against my will, thoughts of Kenya crept into my mind. I wondered what she was doing. Who did she live with? Was she bisexual or lesbian?

Jessie's soft kiss on my cheek abruptly tugged me away from my thoughts. Turning to face her, I closed my eyes and kissed her passionately. She pulled me closer by the drawstring on my sweatpants, and I wrapped my arms around her. We kissed as the waves crashed against the shore. I slid my hands down her back to her behind and then back up again. As we hugged, I felt her breathing on my neck. I inhaled her scent, closed my eyes, and exhaled. I then felt her tongue on my neck. Her right hand found its way to my center. I was only wearing sweatpants and boxers as opposed to my usual jeans, so I felt every intricate detail of her touch against my body.

"Let's go," I said. Not even waiting for her to agree, I moved her hand away from my center and headed back toward her jeep. After putting the key in, I realized that I couldn't wait until we got home. I only turned the key enough for the CD player to play.

"What are you doing?" she asked.

"You," I said and got out. I went to the back and let the backseat down for more room. The music continued to flow through the speakers as we moved to the back. I pulled off my sweatshirt and told her to do the same. She obeyed and in turn pulled my pants and boxers down in one motion. I took them completely off.

Jessie seized control of the situation: first, by looking directly into my eyes, then by sliding her finger inside of me. Feeling her wet in and out took me to another place. She kissed me, and I closed my eyes as she sped up, but then she slowed down and pulled out. The essence of my body flowed out of me as she positioned herself to please me. I couldn't keep quiet. I moaned, and then she moaned. Jessie went from fast to slow, up and down, in and out, around and around, counterclockwise. Damn. I wondered if I would be able to walk when she was finished. Before I could wonder long I felt a vibration. She was wearing her vibrating tongue ring! I remembered the feeling from the first time she used it months before. I squirmed in ecstasy. My breathing sped up, and my heart raced as I got closer and closer to climax.

"Oh, shit—baby—oh—ahh—I'm about to—ahhh—Jessieeee!" The pitch of my voice went higher, and she gave me one strong long lick that ended in a lip-locking kiss to my clit, and I released. I tried to collect myself to return the pleasure, but I couldn't do it right away. Jessie had put it on me, and I was mentally out of it for at least 20 minutes. I sat there with a dumb grin on my face. Then I finally reciprocated before we left the beach parking lot.

The love we made that night was poetic. Submerging into an ocean of lyrics, metaphors, and stanzas, Jessie wrote an erotic epic in the center of my existence with strokes from her tongue. When we got home I could hardly talk. The only word that made sense was, "damn," followed by a smile. It was almost one o'clock in the morning after we showered and finally turned in for the night.

Chapter 16

The next day I did something I hadn't done in awhile. After work at the TV station, I stopped at the gym in our housing community. Jessie had been on my mind all day, and I felt good. It was also supposed to be my last week on the job assignment, but they extended it two weeks. I hoped it would turn into a full-time position.

Jessie and I spoke off and on throughout the day and decided not to do anything really special for our anniversary. The most we would probably do was drive up to Naples for the weekend. And as the day winded down, I left work feeling the urge to work out.

After changing into my sweatpants and T-shirt in the small locker room, I slid my headphones on and listened to inspiring music. I spent a lot of time on my legs using the leg extension and leg press machines in the back then I lifted free weights. After I finished working out and went to buy a drink from a machine in the corner, I saw Kenya.

"Kenya?" I was surprised to see her.

"You remember my name," she said sarcastically.

"Well, yeah, it's just…wait a minute. What are you doing in here?" I asked, then took a sip of my water.

"I live here."

"You what?" I almost spit my drink out.

"I live in the neighborhood, at least for now."

So she was the woman I saw from the window. I didn't know what to say.

"I guess things are better at home for you now." It sounded more like a question.

"They're okay," I said looking down.

"Well, I don't want to keep you." She pulled off her shirt, leaving her in a midnight blue sports bra and gray sweatpants. Kenya had a sexy stomach, but before I had a chance to look at it too much, she turned around and stretched her arms then bent to touch her toes. She turned back around and looked me in the eyes. Kenya licked her lips and smiled. "Are you okay?"

"Huh? Yeah, I'm fine."

"Do you see something you like?" she asked as she stretched her arms behind her back. It was getting hot in that gym. I wiped my forehead, took a sip of water, and tried to play it cool.

"You're all right," I said, "but I shouldn't be looking at you."

"So why are you still here?" she teased. "Hm?"

"I don't know."

"Well, I'll make it easy for you." She looked me up and down. "Erase me from your memory." She turned away from me, and walked toward a treadmill without looking back.

"Wait, wait, wait," I said following her. "What do you mean by that?"

She stopped. "Okay, you have a girlfriend, but there's an obvious attraction between us that maybe we should just leave alone."

I nodded yes, picked up my bag, and turned to leave.

"Bye," she said smiling flirtatiously.

We both knew damn well that wasn't the last time we'd see each other.

As I drove the four short blocks home, all kinds of questions popped into my head. Kenya said she lived in the neighborhood for now. What did that really mean? As for Jessie, was my happiness with her temporary? Would we fade back into a boring routine in a few weeks? Should I call Kenya just to say hello? Why did she have to live so close? Why did she have to be so attractive? Oh, the temptation was real this time. How far away did she live and with whom? Had she seen Jessie and me together? I had to slow my mind down before I gave myself a headache. Damn, she had a beautiful stomach, and her skin was so smooth. Was my memory and estimation right? Were those 36 Cs in that sports bra of hers? Stop! *Get rid of those thoughts, Sadira,* I told myself as I went inside to take a shower. *Get rid of those thoughts.* **Jessie** *is your lover.*

Instead of going to Naples, we decided on a local get-a-way for our anniversary. Jessie and I got a suite at the luxurious Fontainebleau Hilton Hotel on Collins Avenue in Miami Beach. The room was more like a condo, and we ended up ordering room service and talking for most of the night.

"So how are we doing?" she asked a few moments after I turned off the lights to go to sleep.

"What do you mean?"

"Am I getting better? Is our relationship more fulfilling to you?"

Though the answer was yes, Jessie no longer had my undivided attention. Plus, everything was happening so quickly I doubted my thoughts of Kenya would fade. I'd had plenty of opportunities to cheat on Jessie before, but none were like this. "Yeah, I think things are getting better," I finally said. *Liar,* I thought to myself. *Shut up,* I rebutted, being argumentative with myself.

"Well, good," she said. "I want us to move forward. I don't want to lose or hurt you."

"Yeah," was all I said before we snuggled up close to each other and drifted off into a deep sleep.

Chapter 17

"See you later, baby," Jessie said, then kissed me on the cheek and rushed out.

"Don't forget about tonight!" I yelled.

"I'll be there."

A half an hour later I was out the door and on my way to work too. I'd decided to do a poem at Avery's that night. I hadn't been on stage in a while and missed the feeling, plus I really wanted Jessie to be there. I wrote an explosive erotic piece, and knowing me, I'd probably add a little something on the end for her too.

I ended up staying at work later than usual and barely had time to shower and change before going back out. One drawback of my job assignment at the TV station was that it was in West Palm Beach, almost an hour away. I left Jessie a message to meet me at Avery's because one of the guys I worked with wanted to go, but he didn't have a ride. I told him I'd take him, but he'd have to find a way home. He said that would be fine.

"I'll be a little late," Jessie said in a voice mail message, "but I'll be there."

By 8:15 I was at the club relaxing and going over my poems in my mind.

Terry, the MC came over to me. "S. Cooper, long time no see."

"Hey, T, what's going on, man?"

"Good things. The crowd is growing, getting more diverse, things are good."

"Cool."

"Are you going on the stage tonight as our erotic lady?"

"Yes indeed."

"I can't wait. Most of these folks have probably never experienced you. But listen, I need to make sure some things are in order. Here are two drink tickets. Is Jessie coming?"

"Yes."

"All right, I'll see you later."

"See ya."

By 11:00 Jessie still hadn't arrived. When I called, I got her voice mail.

"Yo', S, I'm getting ready to end this set," said Terry "Do you want to go on or wait for the last one?"

"I'll wait."

"Okay."

"Sadira, is that you, girl?" Hearing a familiar voice I turned and saw Devonte dressed in black.

"Devonte! Oh my God, what are you doing here? What's up man?"

"I'm here on a last minute but much needed vacation. I wanted to call you, but I broke my cell phone and couldn't remember your damn number. I didn't have the phonebook I stored in it. How the hell have you been?" He gave me a hug.

"That's no excuse man but whatever. It's good to see you. I've been through a lot, but I'm still blessed." Just then I felt my phone vibrating. "One sec," I said to Devonte and answered the phone.

"Hey, Jess, are you on your way?"

"I'm sorry, baby. I can't make it."

My mood changed instantly. "Why not?"

"I'm on call."

"What? You didn't say anything about working on call tonight, Jess."

"I'm sorry. I promise I'll make it up to you."

"Yeah. See you later." I hung up and turned toward Devonte. "Sorry about that."

"You're still putting up with it," he said shaking his head.

I wasn't in the mood to hear his, 'I told you so.'

"Jessie and her bullshit, right?" he asked.

"Hey, ease up. Not right now. I'm going outside. I'll be back."

"Okay, but you know I warned you a long time ago that I didn't like that girl for you. She's selfish, and her ass never deserved you in the first place."

"Devonte!"

"I'm just saying it because it's the truth. When are you going to wake up? A zebra doesn't change its stripes, Sadira. Anyway, it was good seeing you. We should try to keep in touch after tonight. My numbers haven't changed, and I'm still at WSOL. Look a brother up when you're in the city."

"I will," I said and headed toward the door.

"Hey, S," Terry said. "You're up first in the last set,"

"Okay, I'll be right back."

Just as I stepped outside, I saw three beautiful women get out of a pine green Ford Explorer. I couldn't help but stare, and my eyes widened when I saw that one of them was Kenya. As she and her friends walked by me, we made eye contact. Kenya smiled at me and went inside without stopping.

I stood outside a few moments longer before going back inside.

Terry went to the mic. "The next artist to come up is not a virgin to the microphone, but she has been away for awhile. She usually brings steamy, sex-filled erotica with a twist and for those of you who don't know her, you'll remember her after tonight. So, ladies and gentlemen, I ask you to please direct your love, energy, and attention to the stage for Ms. S. Cooper." R & B music played and people clapped while I walked to the stage.

My eyes met and locked with Kenya's for a brief moment. My first thought was that I didn't want her to hear my erotic poetry, but it was too late. After Terry's introduction I couldn't back out. I had two pieces and the other one was for Jessie, but it didn't make sense to read it without her being there.

"How y'all doing, Avery's?" I asked.

"All right, all right," the crowd responded.

"Good. Well, as Terry mentioned, I go by the name of S. Cooper and the piece I'm going to do for you tonight is actually from a three-part poem called "Sexual Trilogy.""

"And you're only reading one part?" one guy called out. "C'mon, S. Cooper, show us what you've got."

I smiled. "I'm going to read Part Two, so here we go." I cleared my throat, took a deep breath and started…

It's S. Cooper
The super duper lyrical miracle
I'm back for real though, stronger than a 9-inch dildo
I said it before and I'll say it again
Listen, my twist is
I'm here for the ladies
If you ain't got ass and tits you get daps and dismissed
Fellas, y'all better take notes, let's go…

The crowd was like, "whoa." I continued…

With only the light of our fireplace we lay naked relaxing
A thunderstorm CD plays below Maxwell
I'm about to give you a backrub before we head to the bathtub
I ask you to lay on your stomach and you obey, okay
I reach for the heated massage oil
Starting at your feet and rubbing them first
One by one and then up your calves, your thighs, your behind,
And then I let my tongue slide down to follow
I kiss down your legs, suck behind your knees, kiss the bottom of your feet
And baby girl I suck your toes individually
And then back up for your back rub.

I move up to the center of your back
Up to your shoulders and down your arms
On your side I plant wet kisses
Down your spine I drag long licks and
Moan just so you know how far I wanna go.
J t'aime beaucoup,
Oh shoot, I never told you

I speak a lil' French too.
And I'm dyin' to French kiss the lips below your hips
And let my tongue slip, slide and twist your clit into a state of
rapturous ecstasy
But wait...not yet...more 4play before you get the best of me.
I massage your left shoulder with my left hand and your lower
back with my right.
While I tongue kiss the center.

"This Woman's Work" just started playing
I tell you to turn over and you obey me.
Looking directly into your eyes
Makes me wanna say thank you.
I'm grateful to be with you
I used to be so miserable until I stepped to you.
You stole my attention like kleptos do.
But even if you didn't, girl, I would have given it to you.

Kissing your neck while running my right hand down the left side
of your body.
I moan into your ear, then move down to place my ear on your
chest.
Closely I listen and hear your heartbeat.
I concentrate until mine is in sync and you and I become
we...beating together.

One by one I take your breasts into my mouth, sucking and licking,
gently nibbling.
You moan and pull my hair a little.
I can't wait to fill you.
"Till the Cops Come Knockin'" is rocking the room as I move
down your stomach,
Kiss your sides and then move down to the center of you.

The glow of the fire is casting our shadow across the room
Gently I form a triangle with my hands
Massage the exterior of your center

Then kiss your inner thighs
Tell you to open a little wider
And I dive straight inside tongue first
In and out, in and out, then long licks up and down
Then I circle your clit around and round
Speeding up before I slow it down
I close my eyes and get in a zone now
Your juices are steadily flowing down
I'm moving my whole head up and down!

I paused for effect. The crowd was really into it.

The tip of my nose grazes you before my tongue plays with you
Double the feeling. Double the pleasure. Double the fun
It feels like two of me, but baby it's just one!

Moving my tongue with precision, it's my decision
I'm focused on making us both cum harder than a 5-car collision.
You're damn right, I'll cum from just eating you out.
I'll keep going and going in effort to keep you cuming and cuming
At least 5 times in one day
Times 6 days out the week
That's 30 times you're walking wobbly, thanks to me!

The temperature's rising, my finger's inside and
I'm not gonna lie, girl, I'm getting tired
But hearing you scream and moan keeps me wired
I got ten more licks in me now
And about four more kisses
Hear me out, it's been over 120 minutes of pussy eating
Girl, call me two hours of power cause after we cum
We'll take a break and then I'm on my knees for you in the shower.

"Thank you, that's the end of my piece," I told the audience and handed the mic back to Terry.

"Damn," he joked to the audience, "Shit, is my mic still working' or did you melt it with that hot ass piece?"

I laughed, "Naw, man. I didn't mess up the mic."

"Whew," he said.

I heard all kinds of reactions, and they were all good. Some ladies kept clapping and looking at me.

"Is she single and if so, is she taking applications?" one woman shouted out.

Guys smiled and kept applauding too. "Good stuff, S," one man said as I walked off stage.

That's exactly what I wanted, to shock the shit out of them because I'd been out of the loop for so long.

"Now see," Terry said into the mic, "I'm a straight man and you had my attention!" The audience laughed.

"Thanks, T," I told him.

"And on that note," he said, "The next artist to the mic goes by the name of Smooth L."

I went over to the bar and sat down for the rest of the set. Kenya came over to me.

"Interesting piece," she said.

"Interesting?"

"Yeah, it peeked my interest in you even more. You've got skills, Ms. Cooper."

"Thank you."

"You're welcome. So where is your other half, if I may ask?"

"She had to work tonight."

"I see." There was an awkward silence.

"Do you want a drink?" I asked her

"Are you sure?"

"Yeah, why not?"

"Okay," she said and sat down next to me.

I signaled the bartender. "Let me have an Apple Martini," I told him and turned to Kenya.

"And I'll have a Red Devil," she said.

"A what?" I asked.

"Red Devil. Why?"

"Nothing, it's just that… never mind." *Red Devil, that's what Jessie always orders.* It was a mix of vodka, orange juice, sloe gin and peach schnapps "Anyway, I'm glad you enjoyed the poem."

"Yeah, your girl must really be satisfied."

"She's fine." I didn't want to talk about Jessie. "So tell me about yourself."

"What do you want to know?"

"Whatever you're comfortable with sharing."

"Okay, but know that as much as I'd like to stay, I have to leave soon because I'm working early tomorrow."

"That's fine. I'm leaving soon too. What do you do for a living?"

"I'm a doctor."

"What kind?"

"An anesthesiologist."

"Wow, what are you doing living in lil' old Pembroke Pines then, Doc?"

"I'm sort of taking care of a mess my brother made. Plus, this is my first year actually working as an anesthesiologist, so I haven't fully established myself yet."

"You mean, you pretty much drug and numb people up for a living?" I smiled.

"Yes, that's about it. And you?"

"An audio engineer slash freelance photographer."

"That's right. What happened to my shoot?"

"Oh, I'll shoot your ass all right," I joked.

"You promise?"

"Bad Kenya! Bad, bad Kenya," I told her. Whew. I pushed the half glass of martini away from me. I didn't need anymore, plus I was driving home alone.

A beautiful woman came up to us, one that I saw Kenya arrive with. "Excuse me, Kenya? We're ready."

"Okay, Dee," Kenya said, "give me one sec." The woman winked at her and walked back to the table where the other beauty sat.

"Thanks for the drink," said Kenya standing up. "It's time for me to get out of here."

"Yeah, me too." I got up.

"It was nice talking to you," she said to me.

"My thoughts exactly. There are three of you. Who's driving?"

"Oh, Dee is. My car is in the shop."

"Does she live near us? I mean, you?"

"No, actually she lives in…" She stopped in mid-sentence and looked me directly in the eyes as if reading my mind.

I looked at her from head to toe my mind told me to drive home alone or I might end up doing something with her that I'd regret. Kenya was dressed simply enough in a V-neck sweater with fitted jeans and boots, but she seemed to be coated with a sensual power that had me by the neck.

"Well—" I began, but then realized I had to leave before I did something I'd be sorry for.

Kenya smiled. "I'll see you around."

"See you," I said, but neither one of us moved. It felt funny to reach out and shake her hand, so I leaned in and gave her a quick hug. "Get home safe," I told her.

"I will," she said into my ear. I felt the warmth of her breath. *Oh man.* Watching her leave, I exhaled slowly, stood back, and reached in my pocket for my keys. I noticed Terry looking and smiling.

"See you next week?" he said.

"I'll try."

"All right, drive carefully."

"See you later."

When I got back outside it was drizzling and cold, even for Miami. I balled up the piece of paper with Jessie's poem on it and threw it in the garbage. Trying to shield my face from the rain, I walked quickly with my head down to my car.

When I got home, Jessie was asleep on the couch with the TV on. She must have had the heater on hell because it was hot as fuck in the house. I bent down and kissed her on the cheek. "Hey, sleepyhead," I said, "I'm home,"

She blinked a couple times before speaking. "Hey, baby girl," she said, then stretched. "How was it?"

"Awesome! I felt a rush that I haven't felt in a long time." I omitted my disappointment with her and my fascination with Kenya.

"I'll be there next time, I promise."

"Yeah," I paused. "Hey, c'mon, let's go to bed." I helped her up.
She inhaled. "What's that smell?"

"What smell?"

"You smell different." She leaned toward me.

"No, I don't." *What is she talking about? I didn't hug Kenya long enough for her perfume to rub off on me. Or did I?*

"Never mind," she said.

"Okay. Come on, I'm sleepy."

"All right, all right."

The next day thoughts of Kenya streamed through my mind like a classic love song that you wished you could hear at the exact moment of remembering it. She was absolutely gorgeous. No, she was sexy as hell.

A zebra doesn't change its stripes. I heard what Devonte said again in my mind. I missed his crazy ass. He was right, and I hated to admit it. I wondered how different my life would have been had I heeded his advice about Jessie in the first place. I was so in love with the thought of being loved that I settled with Jessie and never looked back, just hoping we would grow together. And we did, but not at the rate or on the path that I think we should have. *Settle.* Should I just admit that I settled?

I did a lot of thinking over the next couple of days, mostly about myself, my issues, and how I could improve. I always knew I was sensitive, but it seemed like the older I got the more my sensitivity increased rather than decreased. Was being too sensitive a bad thing? My feelings could be hurt so easily. I could be like a child sometimes, especially when people broke promises. I hated that.

I also looked back far enough into my past to understand that because as kids Khedara and I were adopted and really didn't have support for anything we did. If there was any support at all, it was Khedara who got it, not me. I was never acknowledged or praised for any activity I did. There was no comforting, no consoling, nothing. I carried that need inside of me into adulthood, and that's why it was so important for Jessie to come to the poetry readings, the parties, the radio station events, or anything else I was involved in.

My problem, I thought, was maybe that I never admitted just how important her support was to me. But was it her fault I have this complex from my childhood? Was it fair of me to expect her to make up for what I missed? Was I asking too much? Was *I* being selfish?

"Sadira?" Jessie said one day, pulling me out of my thoughts.
"Yeah, Jess?"
"What do you want for dinner?"
"Oh, I'm not really hungry."
"What?"
"I just don't have much of an appetite."
"What's wrong?"
"I've just been doing a lot of thinking lately. Jess, do you feel like I pressure you in any way?"
"No, why?"
"I was just thinking."
"What made you ask?"
"Because I was wondering if I maybe make too big of a deal out of you supporting me." As soon as I said it, I immediately wished I could take it back. She was my lady, and she was *supposed* to support me, and vice versa.
"You don't," she said, "and I'm going to try not to miss the next thing."
Try? Thing?
"I mean, I'll be there," she said as if reading my mind.

After we talked a little longer, I told her I wanted to be alone with my thoughts. The more I looked deep inside myself the more I found pain I thought I'd gotten over. How do you know when you're really over something? I mean, you can get over someone in days or months, but how about getting over the emotional damage that's been done to us? Is it possible?
In addition to my abandonment issues stemming from childhood, I thought about the fact that all my relationships ended with my partner leaving. Three of the relationships were with men, and two were with women. One left to follow his dream of playing in the NBA, but he never made it. The other two men gave me the 'it's not you, it's me' speech, and the other two women left for someone more butch. The common factor in each of them was that they all said they couldn't really explain

their leaving because I didn't do anything wrong. Was I unconsciously attracting and choosing people who would reject and hurt me in order to reenact the abandonment I experienced as a child? Did I keep repeating the painful pattern simply because it was familiar?

I remembered once going through a six-month period wondering what was wrong with me. Why did people always leave? But then I thought *nothing lasts forever*—especially not relationships. I put my guard up and went around as if I didn't have any emotions until I met Jessie. Somehow meeting her was the flame that defrosted my frozen heart. Little did I know I'd have to chisel stone from around hers.

I remembered the talks I had with Devonte about Jessie and I thought about those two nights with his cousin, Tricia. What's funny was that part of me knew he was right about Jessie being selfish, but I didn't want to believe it. I had hope. I had hope even though he practically drilled it into my head that Jessie was too self-absorbed for me, or anyone else for that matter. I didn't want to listen then, but I was hearing him now.

Chapter 18

The next day I was in the gym listening to DMX's first CD when Kenya walked in wearing black Champion sweatpants, a crimson sports bra, and a towel slung over her left shoulder. Her hair was under a black head wrap, and she was carrying a bottle of water. Through powerful Sony earpieces music was pouring into my ears. She smiled and waved, and I returned the smile while finishing my workout. As Kenya began to stretch, my eyes followed the rhythmic movements of her body until DMX's barking like a damn dog from the next track on the CD snatched my attention away. With two more reps to go before I would take a break, I closed my eyes and tried to focus. Sensing Kenya's closeness, I opened my eyes to find myself face to face with her.

"Hey, cutie." She softly touched my cheek then moved her hand close to my lips.

It took every bit of strength I had not to kiss her fingers. I stood there, stuck on stupid, as she trailed her index finger over the tip of my nose, my lips, chin, and neck. When she came even closer to me, my breathing got heavier.

"Kenya," I said softly.

She remained silent and looked me directly in the eyes. I swallowed hard as she licked her lips and put her hand on mine. I almost dropped the free weights I was holding. To be on the safe side, I kneeled to put them down. At the moment when I looked up, Jessie walked in.

What the hell is Jessie doing in here? She never comes to the gym. My eyes got wider, and Kenya noticed.

"Are you okay?" Kenya asked sounding concerned.

I played along. "I'm fine, thanks."

"You should get some gloves for weight lifting. It will help your grip," she said.

"I'll do that."

She winked and walked away Just as Jessie came toward me. She and Kenya looked at each other, but didn't say anything.

"Hey, you," I said, wiping my forehead with a hand towel.

"Hi, baby."

"What are you doing here?"

"I left the office early today. It was too stressful. If I didn't leave when I did, I probably would have fired a couple of people."

"Damn, it was that bad, huh?"

"Yeah, I figured you'd be in here."

I glimpsed Kenya behind Jessie. Sweat was glistening on her back. I snuck in one more look before she stepped onto a treadmill.

"Sadira?" Jessie said.

"Huh?"

"Are you almost done working out, or will you be in here awhile?"

"I'm actually almost done."

"Where's your mind at?"

"Here," I lied. I was horny as hell and wanted Kenya in the worst way.

"Okay, well, I'm going to go home. I skipped lunch and I'm starving."

"All right, I'll be there in like thirty minutes or so." Kenya looked our way without breaking her workout. Jessie looked at her, and they locked eyes. When Jessie kept staring, I took her hand to get her attention. *I need to get out of here quick,* I thought. I walked Jessie to her car.

When I reentered the gym, Kenya looked at me and laughed.

"What the hell are you grinning at?" I asked.

"Nothing," she said and laughed. "Your girl is really pretty."

"Thanks, now stop looking at her."

"Oh, I know you didn't go there. Why can't I look at her if you're looking at me?"

I laughed. "You're damn right I went there. I'll thank you now for taking your eyes off my lady. Me and you are a different story."

"She's nice to look at, but not intriguing enough to pursue like you."

"Excuse me?"

"You heard me."

"Hey, don't start any shit."

"Don't worry, most likely you'll be the one to start it."

"Whatever," I said.

"Go on and get back to your workout before Ms. Pretty Eyes comes back to check on your lil' ass."

"Who are you calling little?"

She laughed again. "You!"

"Oh. Well, hey, you're attracted to me though."

"I won't deny that," she said looking me up and down

When I felt my hormones getting the best of me, I knew I had to get away from her. Between Kenya's carefree conversation, the beads of sweat rolling down her perfect stomach, and the tiny piece of red from her Victoria Secret panties that was visible above the waist of her sweatpants, I knew I could lose control.

"Yes!"

"What?" she said.

"I'm going back to my workout. Bye!"

"You sure got excited quick."

"Yeah, I have sporadic Tourettes, you should know that."

"No, you have sporadic punk syndrome. Bye." She licked her lips.

"Blow me."

"Do you have your strap on with you?" she asked with a raised eyebrow.

My jaw dropped in disbelief. *Temptation at its finest,* I thought and shook my head.

"Relax," she said and laughed. "I'm just messing with you. For real, hurry up and get back to your workout so you can go home. I don't want to get you in trouble."

"Yes, I'm going to do that." I walked back over to the Stairmaster, spent five minutes on the machine and then gave up. I was tired, and with Kenya around, I could no longer focus on my workout. I went home.

"Hey!" Jessie said and smiled as soon as I walked in the door. "I know I just saw you, but after the day I had, I just can't wait to snuggle up with you." She gave me a hug.

"Hey, I'm kind of funky, baby."

"I don't care."

I kissed her on the forehead and hugged her back. "Sorry about your day. What did you eat?"

"I just made a sandwich because there were no leftovers, and I didn't want to try to cook anything and have to hear your mouth."

"What?" I asked as we released each other.

"The last time I was going to make breakfast, the first thing out of your mouth was, 'I know you're not cutting that on my counter.'"

I laughed. "Well shit, baby, that's why we have a cutting board. Don't chip up the counter."

"Jerk."

"Yo' mama."

"Don't get your ass whooped, okay? And damn! You do kind of smell like train smoke."

"Train smoke?" I laughed. "You're about to get your feelings hurt in here. I warned you I wasn't the freshest person right now."

She pushed me playfully. "Now you and I both *know* that you might wear boxers, but I run things, okay. You must be feeling yourself right now."

"Whatever."

"Go bathe!" she said, fanning in front of her nose.

I smiled and headed toward the bathroom, leaving a trail of sweaty clothes in the hallway as I peeled them off. "Pick my shit up, now!" I said and went in the bathroom.

When I came out of the bathroom, I saw Jessie curled up on the couch, eating popcorn, and watching cartoons. My clothes were still on the floor.

"Girl, why are these clothes still sitting there?"

"Because that's where you left them."

"You must not want dinner."

"I have a cordless phone and a drawer full of take-out menus."

"You don't play fair."

"I know."

"All right, you got me," I said, picking up my clothes.

"I know I got you."

I sucked my teeth.

"Don't be mad, Sadira."

I ended up cooking dinner as usual. It was nothing elaborate, just fried whiting, brown rice and mixed vegetables.

"Now you know you're doing the dishes, right?" I told her.

"I guess."

"You guess? You better."

"Yeah, yeah."

"I don't know who bit you in the ass today, but don't let me put you on pussy probation, okay?"

"What?"

"You better act right before I revoke your privileges."

She laughed. "Please, you couldn't handle holding out from sex anyway, punk."

"I *can* hold out." My mood changed instantly. I got quiet.

"What's wrong?" Jessie asked.

"Nothing," I sighed deeply.

"You liar, what's wrong with you?"

"I just had a thought, that's all."

"And?"

"As much as you've been working lately, I'm used to going without." I said it with more annoyance in my voice than I intended to.

Her mouth opened at what I'd just said. "Are you serious?" she asked.

I didn't say anything. She was obviously hurt, but it was the truth. When Jessie wasn't going in early, she was working late or on call. I hated her being on call the most because she would just drop whatever she was doing to go fix some company's computer problem. What about my needs?

"I'm sorry," she said.

"Yeah. Hey, let's just go to bed, baby."

"Well, what you said doesn't make me feel good."

"I'm sorry, but that's how I feel. Come on, let's go get some sleep."

We went to bed, and I drifted into a restless sleep until around 3:00 when I woke up to go to the bathroom. When I returned I saw that Jessie was over on my side of the bed. I had no choice but to lie on top of her, right? Right.

"Baby, I'm not really in the mood," she said half asleep.

I got off of her and turned on my side. "Goodnight, Jessie."

"Goodnight."

"Hmph," I said in annoyance.

Silence. She went straight back to sleep.

The next day everything that could go wrong at the station went wrong. And on top of that one of my coworkers decided to show her holiday spirit by attaching bells to her shoes and wrists. Why the hell would someone want to be jingling all damn day? We heard her ass dashing through the fucking halls every time she moved! I had a splitting headache by the time I got off. Ugh. Anyway, it was also open mic night at Avery's, and Jessie wanted to go to make up for missing me on stage the time before. I barely remembered the poem that I wrote for her and ended up throwing it away the last time. *Fuck it.* I planned to read, but I didn't want to do any erotica. I wasn't sure what I was going to read. I just knew I had to do an impressive follow-up my last performance.

When I got home from work I ate and sat down to write a poem for the night. Then I decided what I was going to wear. I was in the shower singing the hell out of "Crazy In Love," when Jessie walked in and caught me butt naked, crooning into a white bar of Dove soap. She didn't say anything. She just shook her head and laughed before walking back out.

By the time we were ready to go Jessie looked absolutely amazing. She had on a black top revealing her cleavage and stomach accented by a pierced navel. She wore leather pants that reminded me of the day we met and some serious heels. I was casual in a Polo sweater and Dockers. It was just one of those nights that I knew before we left the house that all eyes would be on us.

Thoughts of Kenya didn't cross my mind until it was time for me to go on stage. Right after Terry called me she walked in with her friend, Dee. I was the last person in the set.

"Thanks, Terry," I said, taking the mic.

"Whatcha got this week S. Cooper?" one guy asked.

"It better top last week," another said.

"Hey y'all," I said. "I'm actually not doing sex tonight."

I heard groans. "Why not?" someone asked.

"This piece is more of a free-style, plus it's untitled so here we go."

"So how do we know you wrote that poem last week?" someone asked before I started.

"Oh, I wrote it."

"How do I know?" He was leaning back in his chair smiling.

"I'll prove it to you later. Y'all want sex, then I'll ad-lib some if that's all right with Terry." I looked at Terry, and he nodded. I read my poem and was about to step down after I finished when I remembered I said I would do a sexual ad-lib.

"Y'all sure you want this?"

"Yep," a woman said. It was Kenya. "Let's see your versatility."

Damn, I didn't want to do it.

"Go ahead, baby," Jessie said. Kenya looked over at her.

Shit. I took a deep breath, turned around so that my back faced the audience and thought for a minute before turning back around.

"All right. Y'all want sex, then that's what I'll give you. Here we go.

There is nothing special about hittin' every piece of ass that passes by

Anybody can have sex with 100 beautiful women but it takes real talent to find 100 different ways to make love to one woman.

I paused for a moment to think. All eyes were on me.

"Keep going," someone said.

I was uncomfortable, but I didn't want to stand frozen a moment longer with everyone watching. The last thing I wanted was to feel embarrassed so I continued.

"Here's your sex," I said, then closed my eyes to just let the words flow.

When you do get her in the heat of the moment
Undress her slow, then look directly into her eyes
As you lower yourself, kiss down her thighs, calves and gently kiss her feet.

I'm sayin' run your hands up and down the curves of her body
Kiss all over her, back to front, top to bottom, inside and out
Don't stop. Whisper in her ear. Say, baby, cum again and again
and again!
Part her legs, then tongue kiss her there for 3 to 5 minutes
Give her long strong licks
Play lesbian twister with a perpendicular tongue
Intoxicate her without liquor till she gets ridiculously sexually
delirious.
I'm serious no bullshittin' ...

I paused. I wanted to stop even though I got a rush knowing Jessie and Kenya were there.

When I said I wasn't going to continue, the crowd groaned. But Terry ended the set successfully anyway. Jessie had a big smile on her face, and so did Kenya. After Terry closed the set, the DJ played upbeat music, not the usual slow jazzy stuff. Beyonce and Sean Paul's "Baby Boy" pumped through the speakers. I shook a few people's hands before Jessie pulled me onto the dance floor. That was one of her favorite songs to dance to.

I caught Kenya looking at us, but I kept my attention on my lady. After two dances I had to excuse myself to go to the ladies room, which is where I ran into Kenya.

"Nice poem," she said while washing her hands.

"Thanks. I know you know my girl is here tonight."

"Yeah, I saw her."

"Okay, good."

"I won't get you in trouble tonight."

"Tonight? You speak as if it's your ultimate plan."

"It's not really a plan."

"Then what is it?"

"I'm just going to be myself."

"And what is being yourself?"

"Being a flirt, who sometimes gets what she wants."

"And you want me?"

"Yes," she said.

"Knowing I'm unavailable?"

"I won't make the first move, you will."

"But…" I was just about to respond when Jessie walked in. *Oh shit.* I pulled some paper towels from the dispenser and dried my hands.

"Well, I just wanted to say I really liked your poem," said Kenya and turned to walk out.

"Thanks."

Jessie looked Kenya up and down as she passed, and then turned to me. "I was wondering what took you so long."

"Oh, yeah. I got caught up talking."

"You have a new fan I see."

"I guess."

We were silent for a few moments as our eyes met. I looked at Jessie from head to toe, noticing every exquisite detail from her neatly arched eyebrows to her manicured hands, the glow in her blue-gray eyes and the small ring in her belly button. She looked exceptionally beautiful, and I craved her in a way that I hadn't felt in a very long time.

"What's on your mind?" she asked.

"I want to make love to you." Just as I said it loud sound of thunder rattled the night outside the bathroom window.

She smiled.

"What?" I asked.

"I just had a thought."

"And that was?"

"Tight," she said softly.

"Huh?"

"The rain, Sadira. It reminded me of that song you used to sing all the time about standing outside in the rain all night for me."

"Oh, wow. You remember?"

"Mm hm."

"That hasn't changed," I said, moving closer to her.

"Is that so?" I could sense her breathing speeding up.

"Yes…" The door suddenly swung open, and I stopped talking. The two women who came into the bathroom broke the mood.

"Let's go," Jessie said, taking my hand.

As we headed toward the door Terry asked, "Are you ladies calling it a night?"

"Yeah," I said.

"All right, see you next time." He opened the door for us. Kenya and Dee were standing outside.

"That was a nice erotic piece," Dee said. "And I don't even go that way."

"Thanks."

"Real nice," Kenya said. "Will you two be here next week?"

"Um, I don't know. Maybe."

"Okay," she said.

Since it was raining, I said, "Jessie, wait right here. I'm going to go get the car." I made a mad dash through the wet parking lot to my car. I got in and drove to the curb to get Jessie, and we left.

"Do you know her well?"

"Who?"

"Miss Green Eyes," Jessie said in an annoyed tone.

"Kind of."

"What do you mean, kind of?" Jessie sounded irritated.

"Well, I've seen her around where we live. I think she lives in the neighborhood." Of course I knew full well she did.

"What were you two talking about in the ladies room?" she said before I could say anything more.

"Just about my poetry," I said as I merged into the traffic on the highway.

"That's all? If you spoke to her in the bathroom, why did she have to reiterate her feelings again?"

"I don't know."

"Well, I'm just wondering."

"Okay." When I placed my hand on her thigh, she relaxed and rubbed the back of my neck.

"Hey," she said softly.

"Yeah?"

"You've still got it, and your poetry is still great."

I smiled and gave her leg a squeeze. "Thank you, baby."

After we got home and undressed, we climbed into bed and fell asleep in each other's embrace. The sexual hormonal surge that had swept through me earlier had dissolved into a sensual affectionate one, and I was quite content just holding her.

Chapter 19

At 5:30 a.m. the alarm woke us up. That day turned out to be a great day work-wise. I was offered a permanent position at the station and accepted it without hesitation. I called Jessie to tell her the good news, but I got her voice mail so I left a message. After work I went straight to the gym. Jessie and I hadn't had sex in two weeks, and I was frustrated. I decided to work off my hormones in the gym. I felt like I was going to explode.

When I pulled into the parking lot, my cell phone rang. It was Khedara.

"Hey, peanut head," she said.

I laughed. "What's up, sis?"

"You tell me."

"Things are pretty good. I got hired full-time at work today."

"Wonderful! I'm happy for you."

"Oh, shit," I said slowly and was silent. I saw Kenya emerging from the pool area. Little beads of water glistened all over her body, which was covered only by a black two-piece thong set. She walked toward the gym. *Wasn't she cold?* Thank God for tinted windows because the expression on my face was like, Damn! *Look at her ass. There ought to be a law against being so sexy.*

"Sadira!"

"Huh?"

"What are you doing?" Khedara asked

"Nothing."

"You're lying."

"No, I'm not."

"Yes, you are."

"Okay, I just saw Kenya coming out of the pool."

"Who the hell is that?"

"Remember the woman I told you about, the one I met at Walgreens?"

"You kept in contact with her?"

"Not really. I never called, but it turned out she lives in the neighborhood, and she's been to Avery's, plus I see her at the gym all the time."

"Leave her alone, Sadira."

"I didn't do anything."

"*Don't* do anything."

"I won't."

We were silent for a moment.

"Oh fuck," Khedara said and sighed.

"What?"

"Jessie is going to kick your ass."

"I didn't do anything, I told you."

"You're going to."

"No, I'm not," I said trying to convince both her and myself.

"I hope for your own good that you don't."

"Hey, Khedara, I have to go."

"Okay, call me later."

"I will," I said. "Bye."

Now if I was thinking with my brain I would have left the gym and gone home, but I didn't. I grabbed my bag, got out of my car, and went inside. I didn't see Kenya when I first went in, so I changed into my sweats and started stretching. I soon felt a soft hand trail up my spine and straightened up quickly to see Kenya with those bedroom eyes. She'd changed into sneakers, tights, and a sports bra.

"What are you doing?" I asked.

"I'm just saying hi."

"Like that?"

"Well."

"Well what? You better stop."

"Sadira, if you were truly satisfied at home, you wouldn't give me a second thought."

"That's not true. It's in our nature to always want more than we already have. There's no way I wouldn't be naturally tempted by you."

"Remember, you approached me first."

"Yeah, I know. It was a mistake."

"Maybe it wasn't." She looked me straight in the eyes.

I was horny, uncomfortable, and unprepared for this conversation. "Kenya," I began.

"Yes?"

"I like you, okay? Yes, I'm attracted to you, but I have a girlfriend," I picked up two ten pound weights. "And you've met her…well, not really, but you know who she is. I shouldn't have approached you. It *was* a mistake."

"When was the last time she made your toes curl?"

"What?"

"When was the last time she took you out?"

"That doesn't matter."

"When was the last time she sent you a surprise at work or just called to say hi?"

I sighed, and she stepped closer. The only other two people who were in the gym had just walked out. I kept on lifting the weights.

She looked at me seductively, then smiled. "I'm going to leave you alone…for now. You're not the only person who wants me anyway."

"You know, you talk a lot of shit."

"There's only one way to find out." She blew me a kiss. Had she been an inch or two closer her lips would have touched mine. Kenya left thoughts about her branded in my mind as she walked to the back of the gym.

My eyes followed the left and right bounce of her ass like the lady in the Cinnabuns commercial. One bead of sweat was rolling down her spine. Suddenly my cell phone rang. I looked at the caller ID before answering.

"Hey Jessie," I said.

I saw Kenya sitting on the floor with her legs open, as she bent forward and touched her toes. Where was my damn inhaler? Was Jessie on her way to the gym?

"Hey baby, I got your message, congrats!"

"Thanks, where are you?"

"I'm in Hialeah, just leaving a client."

"Whew."

"What?"

"Who? I said 'who'?"

"An accounting firm, why?"

"I don't know, girl. I'm just talking."

"Okay. Anyway, I'll be home around 7:30."

"All right," I said, looking at the clock on the wall. It was 6:15. "What do you want for dinner?"

"Surprise me."

"Surprise you, huh? Okay, I'll think of something."

"Okay, I'll see you later. No, you know what?"

"What's that?"

"I'll bring something home for you as a congratulations for getting the job. What do you want?"

"You, butt naked on a platter."

"Sadira!"

I laughed. "Well, damn it, you asked."

"So what do you want?" I was so caught up in the conversation that I didn't notice Kenya walk up to me. She was a little bit too close for comfort.

"Those cheddar biscuits from Red Lobster."

"Just the biscuits, Sadira?" I heard her laughing.

"No, I mean get me that thing with all the different kinds of shrimp. Fried shrimp, shrimp scampi, garlic shrimp, you know"

"Okay, you want the shrimp combo platter, right?"

"Yes!"

"Why are you yelling?"

"Cause now you have my mouth watering." It was really because Kenya's hand had just touched my left shoulder. "Yes, that's what I want, and the biscuits." I moved away from Kenya so I could concentrate on finishing the conversation.

"Okay," said Jessie, "I'll see you later."

"See you later, baby." I hung up and yelled at Kenya, "Are you crazy?"

"You scared of me?" Kenya asked.

"No. See, this is why I can't mess with you."

"Why?"

"Because if this is how you get me, then this will be how you'd leave me, messing around with some other woman."

She was quiet.

"I thought so," I said.

"Not really," she said. "To tell the truth I wasn't going to use this approach with you, but there's something about your aura that's calling out to my body. I'm sorry. I'm going to step back and let you come to me when you're ready."

"Yeah, all right." She left and sat down to rest.

Twenty minutes later I left the gym because I couldn't take the pressure. I was still on my high from getting the job at the TV station and wanted to do something nice for Jessie for not stressing me while I was out of work. I had temp jobs that really didn't pay much, but Jessie never grumbled or said a word. She held everything together and was strong when I needed her to be. She didn't make me feel less than her, and I appreciated that.

She wouldn't be home by 7:30 if she stopped for dinner, especially not driving from Hialeah. So I figured I had about two hours. As soon as I got in my car, I heard an advertisement on 99 JAMZ for a Maxwell concert coming up in two months. It couldn't have aired at a better time. I immediately called Ticketmaster and got two of the best seats available. *Jessie won't know what to do with herself.* She was totally in love with Maxwell.

After sitting in my parked car for ten minutes, I couldn't think of anything that Jessie wanted that she didn't already have, so I ended up deciding it was time to have a romantic evening. Enough is enough. I needed to feel close to her again. After hearing about the Maxwell tickets Jessie would willingly be my love slave. I had to move quickly though. First, I went to Wal-Mart to find a poster of Maxwell. Then, I went to another shopping center with a Hallmark store and got twenty balloons in every color along with a net. While the saleslady in Hallmark put helium in the balloons, I stepped outside to call Jessie.

She said, "Traffic is a bitch, baby. I'll be there by 8:30 but don't worry. I called in our order so I can just go in and pick it up."

"Okay, cool. See you in a little while."

I went back inside Hallmark, paid, and put all the balloons in my car before hurrying home. I still had to shower and set up our bedroom before she arrived. When I got in, I sifted through my mixed CD's and found two I knew she would like, and put them in the changer. One had a majority of old school and a few not-so-old love songs, and the other had nothing but Maxwell cuts. Then I managed to put the balloons in the net and taped the net to the ceiling so I could easily pull them down later by a string that was attached to it. This was something I always wanted to do, but just never had.

In the bedroom I put some ice and massage oil along with a grape and strawberry fruit cabob on my nightstand. I then placed a vibrator in the night-stand drawer so I wouldn't have to get up and get it later. I put the Maxwell poster in the office. Then, I took a long hot shower and changed into my black silk pajamas that Jessie bought me. I finally heard her pull up into the driveway. I was tired, but I would definitely have energy for the intimacy I so badly wanted with her. I wanted her to feel like a queen even if it took me all night.

"You're ready for bed early," she said when she walked in.

I smiled, kissed her on the cheek, and took her bags from her. For a minute I couldn't speak. I was lost in her eyes, which looked more gray than blue at that moment. I leaned in and kissed her directly on the lips. Finally I said, "I missed you." She smiled and said she missed me too.

I turned on the stereo and the first song to play was "Every Time I Close My Eyes" by Baby Face and Kenny G. As Jessie and I ate dinner, we talked mostly about her workday and the benefits of my new job now that I was no longer a temp.

"You're not allowed in the bedroom until after you shower," I told her.

"What about my clothes?"

"You don't need any. A towel is enough."

She laughed. "Okay then," she said and disappeared into the bathroom.

Cheril N. Clarke

Luther Vandross was playing when she stepped out into the hallway. I pulled her close to me, not to dance but just to hold her quietly as the beautiful lyrics of the love song filled the room. I'd taken off my pajama top and was wearing a black camisole and pants. She opened up her towel and wrapped me in it with her. We kissed until the towel fell, allowing her naked body to pressed into mine. I stretched to flick the hallway light switch off while kissing her. Then Jessie pulled away and got down on her knees. Feeling myself getting weak, I closed my eyes. She pulled my pants down. I wasn't wearing any underwear. My moans mixed with the sounds of the love song that was playing. The feel of Jessie's kisses to my center sent waves of pleasure-filled sensations surging through my body. She swirled her tongue around and around to tease my lips, then licked up and down and slipped inside and back out.

I wanted something to hold on to steady myself, but Jessie pushed my hands back and held them against the wall. As she continued to pleasure me with her tongue and fingers, my body started shaking until I could barely take it anymore. I tried to hold off on my orgasm, but she was making it difficult for me. Her moaning with her mouth completely covering my center gave me a feeling of natural vibration that sent chills through my body. The music seemed to rise with me as Jessie sent me into a shuddering orgasm. After releasing I was breathing fast and heavy. I was definitely ready to give her what she'd just given me to the tenth power.

"Give me your hand," I said and pulled her up. She wiped the essence of me away from her mouth with her towel and followed me into our bedroom.

"Hold on," I told her before opening the door.

"What?"

"You can't look yet." I placed my hand in front her eyes. I opened the door and led her to the bed. Then I helped her lay down and pulled the sheet over her. The room was dark except for two vanilla scented candles.

"No peeking," I told her, and went to the wall that had the string. "Okay, you can look now." I pulled the string, and all the balloons fell down. The glows of red, orange, green, blue, and purple were everywhere. She had a big smile on her face as I closed the door. I told her to lay on her back as I climbed into bed. I reached for the massage oil on my nightstand and massaged her from the back of her neck to the soles of her feet. Then I kissed her body from head to toe before telling her to turn around so I could do it again. I placed soft kisses on her forehead and her eyelids, kissed down her arms and sides, and sucked her fingers— kissing everywhere except her center. She relaxed, closed her eyes, and took deep breaths as I continued to rub her body with my oiled hands. Then I reached for the fruit cabob. It was strawberry, grape, strawberry, and grape on a plastic stick.

The ice had turned to mostly water, but it was still very cool. I dipped the tip of the strawberry in it and used it to slowly and carefully trace her center from top to bottom, inserting just the tip of it inside of her. Romantic music filled the room as I eased the strawberry in and out of her.

"Watch me," I said to her, then ate the fruit that was moist with her juices. She was shocked, but in a good way. Then I opened her legs more, but I put the stick down thinking, *fuck these strawberries.* I couldn't wait anymore so I proceeded to give her a few slow licks before shifting into a more aggressive gear. My tongue felt firm, like it had an erection, and I kept inserting it into her. But I needed room, so I used my elbows to get her to open more because I didn't want to stop to have to actually ask her. Eventually I slowed down and paused in my kissing so I could get to my nightstand and pull out the vibrator. I then licked my way back down her stomach.

"Sadira." She was moaning.

"Hm?"

"Oh, it's just… you feel so good…ohhh…"

I spoke softly. "You feelin' all right?"

"Mm hm," she moaned.

"Good."

I kissed down her legs to her feet and sucked her toes, then made my way back up to her inner thighs. Moving up to her stomach, I placed a soft wet kiss on her navel. She tried to wrap her legs around my neck, but I kept her open so I could slide the vibrator in her while clit kissing so she could feel the circular motion of my tongue as well as the in and outs of six ribbed inches vibrating inside of her. She moaned louder, and soon pulled me up to lay on top of her at full length.

I moved in sync with the rhythm of the music. It seemed like forever since we had been really intimate. My mind wondered while my tongue wandered the geography of her neck in search of the spot that would send her over the top. *Did she really know how much I loved her? Was there even anything that could measure the strength of my love for her?* I was determined not to ruin our relationship by stepping outside of it for Kenya. The feeling of her nails in my back brought me back to the moment, and I sped up and pressed harder. We switched positions and continued until we both released. Jessie collapsed in my arms, and we held each other in a loving embrace.

"You mean so much to me," she whispered in my ear. It caught me by surprise. I still hadn't got used to her sharing her feelings.

I answered her with a kiss before saying, "I have something to show you."

"What?"

"It's in the other room."

"Let's sleep. Show me tomorrow."

"I think you want to see this tonight, Jessie."

"Okay." She put on her pajama top, and we went into the office.

I touched the mouse to bring the computer out of its sleep mode. I'd left it connected to Maxwell's website.

"So?"

"Hold on," I said as I opened up a new window and logged into my e-mail to show her the confirmation of the concert tickets I purchased. Jessie started smiling, then jumped up and down. She was very happy. I showed her the poster that I'd rolled up and said, "Now this is a reminder, if you act up between now and then, I'm scalping the tickets!"

"And get your ass kicked," she said laughing.

"Yeah, yeah, whatever."

"Well, I have something for you," she said. "I was going to give it to you when I first got in, but we got sidetracked with all the sex."

"What do you have for me, woman?"

"Where did you put the bags I came in with?"

"They're in the living room."

"Well, follow me," she said, so I did.

When I opened up a Best-Buy bag and saw the Ipod I yelled "Yeah!" She knew I wanted one of them really bad. "Shit, it feels like Christmas in here."

"I take it you like your gift?"

"Yes, I do. Thank you very much."

"You're welcome."

I didn't want to go to sleep after I got my new toy, but I did. That night was a very good night, and I was very satisfied. *Finally,* I thought, hoping my happiness would last.

Chapter 20

The next two weeks went by smoothly. I didn't see Kenya because my hours weren't consistent. I couldn't always make open mic or the gym at the usual hour. Jessie had been putting in a lot more extra time at work lately, and I noticed a marked change in the chemistry between us. *Maybe she's just tired.* I wished she would take a break and not stay at work so late.

"Hey, Sadira," she said one Sunday night. I didn't even hear her pull up or open the door. I was in the kitchen preparing dinner.

"Hey, how are you?" I asked her as she came into the kitchen.

"Oh, God."

"Stressful day?"

"Yes, it's bad enough I went in on a Sunday."

"I hear you."

"What's for dinner?"

"Nothing special. Salad, baked Ziti, and, um, Sunny Delight. I didn't get a chance to go to pick up more juice."

"Why is that?"

"I spent hours reorganizing my new photos to send to the copyright office."

"I see."

"Are you okay?" I sensed something was bothering her.

"Oh, I'm fine. I'm kind of tired, but that's all. What makes you ask?"

"I was just wondering."

"Oh, I'm fine," she said again.

We ate dinner and watched a Lifetime movie before retiring for the night. Jessie was too tired to be intimate or so she said, so we just went to sleep in a spooning position.

The next day I woke up full of energy. I left for work at 6:00. The day was pretty busy, but it wasn't stressful for the first time in weeks. I went to the gym at what used to be my normal hour, and decided to swim a couple of laps in the pool before starting my workout. It was hot, and there wasn't anyone in the pool area except for a few teenagers who were leaving.

After four laps I got out and headed to the workout area. There was a sign posted noting an early closing at 7:30 instead of 8:30. I was the only one in the gym. After changing into dry clothes, I started with a cardio workout on the bicycle, then went to the machines. I worked my legs, arms, back, and then finally my stomach. In the middle of my second set of sit-ups Kenya walked in wearing a tan sports bra and gray sweat pants. Her hair was wrapped in a black and dark brown cloth. She smiled and waved at me but she didn't come over. When I started on the weights again, I felt sweat running down my stomach and my heartbeat speeding up. *I'm horny and this workout isn't getting rid of the feeling. Damn I want Jessie, but Kenya will surely do. Either one. Anybody, shit!*

"One more set," I told myself. *Be strong.* I struggled through the rest of my work-out and slid down to the floor.

"Are you all right?" Kenya asked.

I nodded yes but sat still. My heart began racing. I looked at the clock. It was ten minutes after seven. *Time to get out of here.* I hardly made it to the door when I started having an asthma attack. It was a frightening battle to breathe. I fumbled with my bag to find my inhaler. Kenya came over.

"My inhaler," I managed to get out while pointing to my bag. I saw worry on her face. She looked in my bag, but couldn't find it. I braced myself with one hand on the wall.

"Car," I told her as I felt my energy disappearing.

"In your car? Which one, Sadira?"

I gave her my keys. We were the only ones there, so there should only be two cars out front. "My glove compartment," I gasped.

She left and time felt like it was moving in slow motion before she rushed back in. "Here, hurry up!" she said handing me my inhaler. "Hurry up, Sadira, use it."

One good pull and my lungs opened up. I could breath. Damn, I was tired. I tried to get up, but I couldn't.

"Just relax," she told me. "Take deep breaths."

By then I was sitting on the floor with my back against the wall, and she was kneeling down beside me with her hand on my shoulder. There was concern in her eyes.

"Are you thirsty?" she asked me.

"Yeah," I said softly.

"I'll be right back." she got up and went off to the vending machine.

My phone beeped and notified me of one missed call. I didn't even hear it ring. When I dialed into the voice mail, I heard Jessie's voice. "Baby, I'm working late and won't be home until 9:30 or 10:00. I'm sorry." I pushed 7 to delete the message and hung up.

Kenya came back to me with a bottle of water. "How are you feeling?" She kneeled back down and handed me the bottle.

"Better now," I said, locking my eyes on her.

A guy said, sticking his head in the gym. "Closing soon," then disappeared.

"Hey, Kenya, thanks for helping me."

"No problem. I'm glad I was here. I didn't know you had asthma. You should always have your inhaler with you, Sadira. What if you were alone?"

"I know, I know. And there is a lot you don't know about me."

"Hm, I always like research assignments." She smiled and got up.

I stood up and slung my bag over my right shoulder. "It's time to get out of here."

"Yeah."

I waited around for Kenya to grab her gym bag so we could walk out together. The streetlight was out, so the parking lot was dark except for the stars. As I walked to my car, I realized she hadn't given me back my keys. A black convertible Saab was two spaces over from me.

"That's your car?"

"Yes, it is."

"Nice," I said, then paused. "Um, can I have my keys back, please?"

"Oh, sure." She came over to me, and her fingers touched mine. I took her hand, and we looked into each other's eyes. I leaned back against my car, and she took a step closer.

"Thanks," I said softly. When she moved in to kiss me, I didn't stop her. Finally our lips met. I closed my eyes and pulled her body into mine. Our kissing became aggressive, and our tongues became active exploring each other's mouth. Seconds after I put my left hand on the small of her back, Kenya's ringing cell phone jolted us of our kiss.

"Oh, shit," was the first thing out of my mouth. Kenya backed away and answered her phone. "Hello?"

It felt funny listening to her one sided conversation.

"Oh, hey, I'm on my way now."

Did I hear her right? There was a touch of flirtatiousness in her voice directed to the person on the phone. She laughed and smiled before she ended the call. I stood there with my feelings hurt and jealous.

"Are you okay?"

"Yes, I am," I lied. I had no right to be jealous, but couldn't help it. It was time for me to go home.

Without saying anything Kenya pulled me back to her and kissed me hard and passionately for several minutes before we stopped. My breathing sped up, and my heart was pounding. I was so damn horny. We stared at each other under the quiet blanket of the starlit night.

She looked at her watch. "Shit, I have to go."

I grazed her center with two of my fingers. "Kenya, I know you have to go. Thanks for helping me tonight."

"Mm, no problem." She then placed her index finger on my lips before walking to her car. "Shh."

Kenya left, and I pulled out right behind her. The first thing I did when I got home was take a shower. Thoughts of being intimate with her flooded my mind as the warm water splashed against my skin. I imagined her beautiful body dripping with water, soapsuds sliding down her curves, her nipples erect. *Stop it,* I told myself.

I got out of the shower, ate, and just sat around. The house was deadly quiet. I went into the bedroom and dozed off waiting for Jessie to come home. I slept longer than I expected, and woke up when I heard her shuffling around in the bathroom.

"Hey you," she said when she came in the bedroom.

"Hi. How long have you been here?" I said, getting up.

"Not long," She kissed me on the cheek.

"You look beat."

"I am tired. I'm going to take a personal day soon so I can get some rest. Anyway, I missed you. How does a back rub sound?"

"From who?"

"Um, me. Who else?"

"Sounds good. You sure are being extra sweet to me tonight."

"Don't start with me. Either you want me to work on being sweeter or go back to how I was when you complained."

"All right, all right. And don't get too loose with the talking. Remember, the Maxwell concert is one week away, and I will sell your ticket!"

"Oh, give me a break. Lay your ass down so I can hook you up."

I laughed and pushed her playfully before lying down. As she massaged my shoulders, neck and back, I closed my eyes and thought about Kenya's naked body.

"How does it feel, baby girl?" Jessie asked.

"Good."

"Are there any specific spots that you want me to go back to?"

"Mm, just keep doing what you're doing."

After awhile I returned the favor and gave her a complete body rub. I wanted to have sex, but it felt funny because I didn't want to have it with Jessie. I really wanted Kenya. I lay down next to her after I finished.

"You're quiet tonight," she said.

Before she could say anything more, I kissed her. I didn't ease up until she was on her back and I was on top of her. My hands traced the curves of her body as I kissed and sucked on her neck.

"Baby, I'm tired." She looked me in the eyes.

"Please, Jessie, please. I need you."

She sighed then smiled "You horn toad! Come on." Jessie kissed me. There was no more talking that night. I did what I had to do to give me time to get my shit together.

The next day I did some serious thinking. I knew I needed some space, but I wasn't basing it on the fact of desiring Kenya. I needed space because I messed up big time with Jessie. From the beginning of our relationship I pushed it, then stayed in, ignoring the gut feeling I had all along because I wanted to be with someone. *Now I'm frustrated and unsatisfied.* Jessie is coming around, but it's too late. I'd already violated her trust by secretly desiring and kissing Kenya.

I didn't make it to the gym the next day, but it was open mic night at Avery's. Jessie had already told me she couldn't come, which was okay because I didn't plan on going on the mic. Kenya was there and alone at the bar.

As I walked toward her, I said, "Hi." *Why are you approaching her?* I asked myself, but proceeded anyway.

"Hey. I didn't expect to see you here tonight."

"Well, I just came for an hour or two to listen." She looked a little sad. "Are you okay?"

"Yeah," she said with a sigh. "I'm okay."

"You're lying, but I'll let it slide. If you want to tell me what's wrong, you can."

"It's family stuff. My older brother is the biggest kid. But anyway how are you doing? Are you alone?"

"Yes, Jessie is working as usual, but I'm fine."

"I see. Do you want a drink?"

"No, that's okay." *Damn, she looks good.*

Terry walked over to us. "What's up, S?"

"Hey, man. I'm feeling all right. How are you?"

"Inspired as usual. I'm sorry," he said, looking at Kenya, "I'm Terry."

She extended her hand and smiled. "Kenya."

He looked at me with curiosity, then said, "I'll see you around, S."

"See you." I knew what he was thinking, and I was glad he didn't bring Jessie up.

After clearing my throat I said, "Kenya?"

She looked me up and down and seductively bit her bottom lip. "Yes?" She took a sip of her drink.

"Do you want to get out of here?"

"What?"

"I'm asking if you want to leave—to talk."

"Just talk? We can talk here, Sadira."

"I know, but I'd like some privacy. There are too many familiar eyes on me in here."

"Okay, let me finish my drink, and we can go."

I didn't know what the hell I was thinking or what would happen, but it was too late for me to turn back. *Is it really?* my conscience asked. I excused myself and went to the ladies room while Kenya finished her drink.

When I walked back to her, I said, "Let's take my car."

"Where we going?"

"I'm not sure yet, but we can at least sit inside until I figure that out."

When we got in my car she said, "Nice car."

"Thanks."

"Okay, so what do you want to talk about?"

"Anything. I'm an open book. Are you?"

"Yeah, I'm open. So…" Her voice trailed off into silence.

"Are you seeing anyone seriously right now?" I asked her.

"Not really. I'm trying to steady myself with my work. I'm not sure if I'm going to be in Miami that much longer anyway."

"Why?"

"I'll tell you another time."

"What happened to being an open book?"

"Just act like a page is missing."

"Fine." I sighed.

"What's wrong?"

"Just wondering. Why am I here…with you when I have a girlfriend?"

"It's because you're missing something, Sadira. I can't tell you what it is, but that's why you're here with me."

I did not deny what she was saying.

She looked directly at me. "What are you missing at home?" Kenya possessed a certain feminine power that radiated from her inner being. When she spoke it was magnetic. Her voice, which vibrated with the strength of a god, gently reeled me in.

I paused for a moment before speaking. "Well, the affection that I thought I was missing I'm now getting, but it's still not enough. It's too late. I made mistakes a long time ago that I'm paying for now."

"What kind of mistakes?"

"Just ignoring signs."

"I see." Our conversation stopped.

I turned the car on and then some music to break the silence. "Let's just drive around for a bit." "Then I'll bring you back to get your car."

"Okay."

"Come here," I said before driving off.

"What?"

"Come here," I said again. When she leaned over, I placed my right hand behind her neck and kissed her. She didn't stop me at first, but then pulled back.

"Hey," she said. "I know I came on to you really strong, but I really want you to think about what you have on the line before we…you know…" Her eyes had an unforgettable glow.

"Yeah I know." When I put my car in drive, I accidentally banged my head against the soft headrest before heading out. *Shit.*

We drove up 95 and back down to Avery's. On the drive I shared with her all of what I was feeling and the mistakes I'd made. She told me more about herself too. She was taking over the payments on a townhouse her brother almost lost through foreclosure.

Kenya's last relationship had ended three years before while she was in medical school. Talking with Kenya was different than with Jessie. A lot of times Jessie only listened enough to formulate her response. Kenya paid attention to detail, and seemed to know exactly what to say and when to say it. Her aggressive femme attitude that I'd gotten used to was now a softer, laid back, more inviting personality. When we got back to Avery's, I pulled up next to her car. We sat for a little while longer before calling it a night. Kenya and I had talked so much driving around that my hormones had a chance to calm down. Just as she was getting out of my car, Jessie called me and asked what time I would get home.

"I'm actually leaving now," I told her.

"Okay, I'll try to wait up for you, but I'm sleepy."

"Go on to sleep, Jess. I'll be home in about a half an hour."

"All right."

"Bye."

Standing at the door, Kenya looked at me and smiled. She shook her head. "I'll see you around, Sadira." She blew me a kiss and went to her car.

"See you."

When I got home, Jessie was asleep. I took a quick shower and changed into my pajamas. The last time I was close to Kenya, Jessie said I smelled different. I didn't want to give her reason to start suspecting foul play. *Keep it clean and stay cool.*

"Hey," she mumbled when I came in the bedroom.

"Hi, Jess."

"How was it?"

"It was cool."

"That's good." I got into bed, and she backed up into me. I kissed her on the back of the neck and tried to go to sleep, but again I kept thinking about a naked Kenya moaning from the pleasure I could give her. Damn.

Chapter 21

The next two days went by smoothly. I didn't see Kenya because my work hours changed again. Jessie and I went to the Maxwell concert and had a great time. We came home with all kinds of pictures and souvenirs.

The minute we got in the house passion mixed with adrenaline took over. In the bedroom, we skipped the foreplay. Still fully clothed, kissing, groping, grinding, grabbing, smacking, and moaning, we couldn't wait to just flat out fuck. She unzipped my pants while I unfastened her shirt. We couldn't get undressed fast enough.

"Lay on your back," I told her, and she complied. My tongue and hands explored the contours of her figure before reaching her center. I really don't know how much time passed while I was down there, but it was quite awhile. After her climatic release she pulled me up to return the favor.

I climaxed quickly, but it didn't take long for me to get charged back up for another orgasm. Jessie and I changed positions so that I was on top again, moving rhythmically into her upward thrust. We had no additional helpers. Everything was natural. Body to body, wetness to wetness, and breasts to breasts had me on the razor-sharp edge of climax number two. The faster I went, the more of a sweat I worked up. Our moans got louder and louder until soon Jessie was screaming my name. All that could be heard between the two of us were oohs and ahhs.

"Jessie, oh shit…oh…Oh…"

"Yes…yes…ahhh… baby…" She wrapped her legs around my waist and arms around my neck. My face was buried in her neck in between talking.

"How you feelin'?" I asked her, almost out of breath. "You like it? You feel me?"

"Yes, baby, yes!"

"Yeah?"

"Hm hm." As the pitch of her moans rose, my heartbeat sped up. Our bodies seemed to be slipping, sliding, and passionately colliding into each other. I closed my eyes and got deep in a zone. She came again, and I was moments away from another climax.

"I'm on my way, baby," I told her.

"Go ahead and let it out. Come on!" Her nails were in my back, and she was licking on my ear.

I came right before she said, "Oh shit, I'm about to cum again. Yes…oh, oh Oh…baby…Kenya."

Everything stopped. I was stunned. The room was silent. I looked at her in disbelief. "What did you say?"

"Um." She had a worried looked on her face. "I said…" Her voice trailed off.

I didn't want her to answer my question because I knew it would be a lie. As pain and anger rose up inside me, I got off her and asked again, "What did you just say?"

"Wait, wait, wait, you…you didn't hear me right," she stuttered.

"I, I, I didn't hear you right? You called me Kenya! What the hell is going on in here?"

"Sadira, hold on, I can explain."

"You can explain? You can…" I couldn't finish talking. I was devastated. My mind was so messed up. I didn't know what to do. Plus, I wondered how much could I complain, considering I kissed Kenya and wanted to sleep with her too? But I didn't! How could she?

Jessie reached for my hand, but I pulled back.

"Don't touch me!" I yelled. I thought back to the night they were together outside of Avery's while I was getting the car, and how inquisitive Jessie was about her. What was that about? I thought about how I kissed Kenya, and she kissed me back. Oh, that trifling bitch! She fucked my girl! Was Kenya on the phone with *Jessie* right in front of me the other night?

"You slept with someone else." That was all I could get out. I kept shaking my head.

"I didn't mean for this to happen," she said weakly.

"Shut up! I don't want to hear anything you have to say, Jessie!"

"Wait," she pleaded.

I started putting my clothes on. I didn't even want to look at her.

"What are you doing? Where are you going? Sadira, just listen to me, please."

I ignored her and walked toward the door. She grabbed my arm.

"Back the fuck up!" I said, pushing her off me. I walked to the living room to get my keys. I didn't know where I was going, but nothing good would happen if I stayed at home. Jessie followed me, still begging me to listen, but I didn't want to hear anything she had to say.

"I know you're upset, but would you just listen to me, please?" She stood in front of the door.

"Move," I told her, but she stayed put.

"Sadira, listen. I don't want you to go. Please, I made a mistake. She doesn't mean anything to me. If you would just let me…" She pulled at my hand again, but that only enraged me more.

"Get the fuck out of my way!" I yelled. She looked at me startled. There was pain on her face. Then she started crying. I rarely raised my voice, much less lay a hand on her in a way that wasn't affectionate. Now that she realized things had changed with me, she was reduced to regretful tears.

"I'm sorry," she said softly. "I'm so sorry. I never meant to…"

"Just get out of my way." My own tears were battling to come out, but I fought them back. I pushed her aside and opened the door.

"Come back!" she pleaded.

I didn't answer her. I just walked out and left. I didn't have my keys, so I was on foot. *You should always have your inhaler with you, Sadira.* I remembered Kenya saying. In my rush to get out the house, I forgot the damn thing. Kenya? *Where the hell did she live anyway?* It was cool out as I walked down my block. All kinds of thoughts ran through my mind. *How did Kenya and Jessie end up together? Did Jessie already know Kenya before she told me she didn't like her? How long had she been seeing her and when? Was it just sex or was there an emotional connection? How much did Kenya know about me through Jessie? Did Jessie tell her about our sex life?* Questions darted through my mind as thick drops of rain started to fall.

I decided to walk to the store and buy a pack of Djarums to smoke. I hadn't touched a cigarette in years, but now I was suddenly craving one. Jessie would have a fit if she knew. *Oh fuck Jessie!* As the rain fell harder, I could no longer hold my tears. I knew that crying in the rain only camouflaged tears. It did not get rid of the pain. Oh, how I wished the skies had the power to wash my pain away. *How could this happen? When?* I walked around aimlessly before going to the store. Running my hands over my head in pain and confusion, I felt out of control. My world was closing in on me. I wanted to get out, to break free of this never ending cycle of pain! Unable to stop my tears or control my feelings, I thought I was going to have a nervous breakdown. *I have to work late…I'm on call…I'm too tired tonight…I'm sorry, baby.* Jessie's words echoed like gunfire in my head, and suddenly I felt like a big fool. Working late? She was fucking around on me. "That cheating bitch! Here I am trying so hard to be faithful and strong!" I said out loud as the rain drenched me. My head was beginning to ache.

As I crossed the street to head to the store, I saw Kenya's black convertible Saab in the parking space of the corner house. There was one light on in the house, so instead of going to the store, I went directly over to that house. I knocked on the door as the heavy raindrops continued to crash down on me. There was no answer. I knocked again and rang the doorbell. A few moments passed before the door was finally opened. Sure enough it was Kenya, who was draped in a towel with her hair wrapped.

"What are you doing here?" She looked very surprised.

"You slept with Jessie."

"What?"

"You slept with Jessie!" I yelled.

"Okay, first of all, calm down."

I wanted to stop my crying, but I couldn't. The tears slowed down, but they didn't stop. My eyes were burning. "Kenya, tell me the truth."

She sighed. "Yes, I did sleep with her a few times."

It felt like a hammer had been slammed into my heart. I was surprised I didn't collapse. I didn't even have the strength to fight her.

"Calm down and come inside if you want answers," she said in a calm voice. She stepped back and opened the door for me to enter.

Standing in her living room, I shook my head. "How could you fuck my lady and smile in my face the whole time? How could you sleep with her and then try to fuck me? What the hell is wrong with you?"

Kenya was standing in front of me. "We've been sleeping together for the last month, and she wanted it," she said matter-of-factly.

"You're lying. You're a liar!" I felt my anger beginning to boil. She stood her ground and didn't move. "Tell me the truth!" My chest was tightening with pain.

"Why would I lie to you, Sadira?"

"Why would Jessie want to sleep with you?" I was suddenly sorry I asked. I was afraid of what her answer might be.

"Why did you want to sleep with me?"

I did not speak. My tears started flowing again. I didn't want to believe it.

"Do you want to know what happened?"

"No." I only wanted to get out of there.

When I went to the door, Kenya shouted, "Sadira, I really didn't intend to sleep with her."

I turned around enraged. "So you just fell in her pussy by accident?"

"Actually," she said with a mischievous look, "her face went in mine."

The nerve of this woman! I raced toward her and went to slap her in the face, but Kenya caught my hand.

"Shit, bitch, are you crazy? You fuck my girl and tell me to my face that she ate you out? You must have lost your damn mind!" I pulled my arm out of her grip and pushed her against the wall.

"If you came here to fight me, Sadira, you better know what you're getting yourself into!" She had a vicious look on her face.

My thoughts were scattered. I'd never experienced a pain so deep in my life. At the drop of a dime I would have willingly given my last breath for Jessie. Kenya managed to destroy all that we had built.

I pushed her against the wall again, harder this time. Her towel fell off her, and when she tried to cover herself, I slapped her across the face. She looked stunned and disoriented.

"I can't believe you! What kind of sick, twisted bitch…"

She lunged at me and grabbed me around my neck with both hands. She forced me down to the floor. Still naked, she pressed her knee into my stomach and yelled, "What are you going to do?"

"I'm going to kill you," I gasped trying to breathe as she choked me. I dug my nails into her hands to try to loosen her grip, but that didn't work. Then, I managed to reach my hand up, grab a handful of her hair, and pull as hard as I could. I held on and pulled her head almost down to my level. She screamed and let go of my throat long enough for me to quickly flip her over. Now our positions were reversed. I was on top of her holding her arms down with my knees. I punched her in the face, but then I lost my balance and she got loose. We rolled around on the floor, each trying to get the upper hand. When we were both on our sides facing each other with our hands full of each other's hair, we locked eyes in a fierce stare. Then she moved her head toward me and kissed me on the lips.

"Bitch, don't you fucking dare!" I screamed in disbelief.

"Shut the fuck up!" she said forcefully and kissed me again, this time pressing her naked body against mine.

All of the anger, all of the pain and confusion, everything was surfacing. It turned my rage into a violent passion. Holding her tight and letting the sexual energy flow, I kissed her back. Kenya grabbed me hard, letting her nails go into my back as I moved on top of her. I quickly got control of myself and stopped.

"Get your ass up," I told her.

She smiled devilishly, and we stood up. Moments later we were up against the wall and all over each other. Kenya unbuttoned, then unzipped my jeans, and the next thing I felt was one of her fingers inside of me. After a few strokes I stopped kissing her. She slowly pulled out and leaned back.

Everything about her looked enticing. Her hair was pulled back, her stomach was tight, and her breasts perky and nipples erect. She slowly guided her hands up and down her own body until she reached her neatly shaved center. Looking me directly in the eyes, she inched up on her toes, tossed her head back, and fingered herself in front of me with her right hand while her left hand caressed her own breasts.

I moved closer to her, kissed her neck and eased my index finger inside of her. Our fingers touched. I'd never done a double fingering before. It was a crazy turn on.

"Mm hm." We continued awhile longer before pulling out. Kenya then took my hand and sucked the finger that had been inside of her.

She grabbed me by the pants and led me to her bedroom. Her room had a California King sized bed covered in red sheets. I heard rap music playing. She threw stuff off of the bed, and my eyes became fixed on her ass as she crawled into the bed.

I forced her legs open and kissed her voraciously. Then I planted myself full-length in between her legs and moved in a wavelike motion. Kenya matched me, thrust for thrust. We were making the headboard bang against the wall as rap music played. It fit the violent sex we were having. The entire bed was moving. I sped up and moved harder and she did the same. We got wet and slippery, our rough movements caused the fitted sheets to come loose. My adrenaline was flowing. Kenya was not at all like Jessie, and it made a hell of a difference in my performance.

"Say my name, bitch," I told her. I was in a zone.

"Sadira!"

"Scream it!"

"Sadira! Oh, yes! If you want the pussy, then take it. Write your name on it. Yes, baby, bang me."

Her earlier forwardness was a thin covering for the true crazy freak that was within her. After awhile I slowed down to pace myself. There was no way in hell it was going to be over too quickly. Kenya and I changed positions and she rode me. Her head was back, her breasts were out, and I could feel her wetness oozing into me as she moved. I let her continue so I could rest, then I took charge again. This time I got rougher. She pulled the sheets, then she pulled my hair, and we both screamed obscenities with great pleasure. We climaxed simultaneously.

"Turn around," I told her.

"What?"

"I said, turn your ass around."

She did as I said. Then I kissed down her spine to her behind, let the tip of my tongue trace down and back up before I smacked her a couple of times. *Jessie never let me do that.* My mind was all over the place though my body was with Kenya, who enjoyed it and encouraged me to be as sexually free as I wanted to be. I was rough enough with Kenya to ensure she wouldn't be able to walk straight the next day. I'd gone through so much shit with Jessie, I deserved some new pussy, even if it was from Kenya. I just didn't give a fuck anymore. We continued unleashing our sexual aggression from different positions, including 69 until the sheets were completely wet and we were totally exhausted.

Minutes later her phone rang, but she didn't answer. We didn't speak. I turned my back to her and stared at the wall. "I'm about ready to leave now," I finally said.

She looked at me as if she didn't want me to go, but I knew I had to go home sooner or later. She kissed me on the lips without tongue and simply said, "Okay."

"That really was…" I began to say when I heard the door open.

"Are you expecting somebody?"

"No."

"Your brother?"

"No, he's out of town."

"Kenya?" a female voice called.

It was Jessie. I got up quickly and Kenya moved toward the bedroom door, and pushed it shut, but Jessie's voice was already getting louder.

"Who is it?" Kenya asked as she rushed to put clothes on.

My first reaction was anger that she showed up. I told myself, *You can't get too mad at her because you were in Kenya's bed after finding out she slept with Jessie!*

"It's Jessie," said the voice on the other side of the door. "Your door was unlocked. Look, Sadira found out and she left. We have to talk, Kenya." Her voice was a mix of anger and sorrow.

"Hold on a sec. I'll be right out," Kenya said, putting on a robe, but it was too late. Jessie opened the door and walked in to see us both half dressed in the middle of a room that distinctly smelled of sex. The bed looked like a hurricane hit it. It was obvious what happened. I didn't have time to fix my clothes, so I just stood there tired and watched in horror as Jessie sank to her knees and bawled. Kenya was unperturbed. It puzzled me how she could be so calm and collected in the middle of it all.

What did I just do? I thought. Hearing Jessie wailing made me cry too. I wondered how Kenya felt inside. In one night she reduced both of us to tears. There was a lot of pain in her house. It hurt me deeply to see Jessie crumble like that in front of me.

"Oh, God!" said Kenya. "You know what? I just had a couple of *incredible* orgasms and I *cannot* take all this drama." She waved her hand in disgust and walked out of the room. I was too concerned with Jessie to react to Kenya's effrontery, so I turned my attention back to Jessie.

I wondered if she and I could grow from this or if the damage would be irreparable. *I want us to be together.* I wondered how realistically we could make things work. *You just tore whatever thread of hope was left for you by fucking Kenya.* I needed time to figure things out.

It was raining hard outside when I left Kenya's house. Jessie walked ahead of me, but I didn't hurry to catch up with her. I didn't cry. I just walked home with my head down and my hands in my pockets.

Chapter 22

By the time I got home I was drenched, and I was sneezing and coughing. I wasn't even sure of what time it was. *It's probably around five in the morning.* The sun would be coming up soon. Jessie, whose eyes were red, started to speak but stopped. She didn't know what to say, and neither did I.

I walked inside and stood by the front door in silence. When Jessie hesitantly reached for me, I didn't move toward her. She pulled back, then hugged me and cried on my shoulder. I was dripping water all over the floor, and my arms were by my side not returning her hug. The only movement that came from me was a cough.

"I'm sorry, Sadira. I feel like this is all my fault."

"Shh," I said, finally putting my arms around her waist. She held me tight even though I was wet.

"Come on and get out of those clothes," she said.

I took off my shoes, then went to the bathroom and peeled off my wet clothes. Leaning forward, I braced myself on the sink, and looked in the mirror. I didn't even recognize myself. I put my head down and shook it in disbelief at all that happened. Soon Jessie knocked on the door.

"Do you need anything?"

"No, I'm going to take a warm shower. Then we can talk."

"Okay."

I cried like a baby in the shower. Everything was so messed up, and I felt hurt in a way that I'd never felt before. It pained me even more to realize that I did it to myself. There was no one for me to truly blame but me. I didn't know Jessie's reason for cheating and still wasn't sure if I wanted to know. All I knew was that I could no longer live in the ignorant bliss of pretending everything between us would be okay. We violated our relationship from both sides. I'd wanted so badly for us to be a story with a happy ending, but what's a story without conflict?

I left the bathroom and went to the bedroom where I found Jessie sitting on the bed staring at me with hopeful eyes.

"Hey," she said, then sighed.

"Hi."

An uncomfortable silence filled the room as I stood wrapped in my towel. I noticed Jessie had laid out dry clothes for me, but I was in no mood to share the bed with her.

I sat down. "So?"

"I'm so sorry, Sadira. I made a terrible mistake."

When I bit my bottom lip and closed my eyes, the thought of Jessie going down on Kenya crossed my mind. I didn't know if I should let Jessie explain herself or not. I was crushed and confused.

"I don't want to know any of the details of you and Kenya," I told her.

"You don't?"

"No, I don't." I looked up at the ceiling as if waiting for a divine ray of hope to speak to my soul and help me out of my dilemma. Just as I started to speak, the phone rang, but Jessie picked up before me.

"No, Khedara it's okay. Thanks. She's home, and we're talking right now. I'll have her call you later."

The room was silent. Jessie started to cry softly, and her skin seemed to turn pale. She brought her knees to her chest and folded her arms, then lowered her head and sobbed. I put my hand on her arm, but she just kept crying.

"Jessie?"

"Yeah?" she said without lifting her head to look at me.

"Jessie, listen. I made a mistake too. I wish I could say that it was in retaliation, but I can't. Well, maybe it was a mix."

"What are you talking about?"

I was silent.

"What do you mean?"

"I mean that I've been attracted to Kenya for months now, but I never acted on it until tonight." I watched the hurt build up in her eyes, but she didn't say anything.

She sighed. "Well, I foolishly acted on my initial attraction."

I felt pain shoot through me.

"I regret sleeping with her," Jessie said.

Funny, I wasn't sure if I did. I wondered if it were really a heat of the moment situation or more of an excuse, a chance to get something that I'd wanted for so long.

"I was going to stop," she said. "Oh my God, I feel so stupid." She buried her face in her hands and cried uncontrollably.

"I'm sorry, Jessie" The tables had turned. This time when I tried to touch her she flinched. For several minutes she didn't say anything that was audible.

The sun crept into the sky allowing light to seep through the blinds. I don't know how I managed to remember, but I called my job to let them know I wouldn't be in and I called Jessie's assistant too. The unexpected sounds of our clock radio startled me, and of all songs to be playing it was a song by Jaheim called "Backtight" that I always used to sing to Jessie.

I closed my eyes and held back tears. Memories of the good times we shared drifted through my mind—curled up on the couch, joking around, the beaches, the quality times at open mics, the Fontainebleau. I remembered the good times and smiled. It all flashed before me like jagged scenes of a love story. I would do anything to fix our relationship, even if it meant time apart or counseling. Amid all of the pain and bitterness that had been generated there was still a ray of hope. I needed Jessie.

She looked at me, but didn't say a word. Her eyes told me the song had jarred memories for her too. Music had always been one of the driving forces in our communication. It helped us connect. When neither of us could speak, the melodies of love songs spoke for us.

"Do you love her?" I finally asked her.

"No, Sadira, I only love you. I have only loved you." She took a deep breath and gripped the sheets. Looking at me, she said, "So I guess Kenya gave you what I couldn't?"

I paused for a moment before speaking. "What is it that *you* were missing, Jessie?"

She remained silent.

I sighed and took her hand. "For me Kenya was a release, an outlet. Something I got out of my system. I no longer desire her. All she did was make me realize how much I wanted to make things work with you." I watched her nod understandingly. "Kenya was an illusion, a mirage, a temporary solution for a long-term problem for me. I don't know about you." Letting go of Jessie's hand, I looked at her and waited for her to speak.

We shared a long silence. For a few seconds I flip-flopped my earlier decision about not wanting to know the story of her and Kenya, but it hurt me so bad just to think about it that I decided that I really didn't want to know what happened between them. Some things are better left unsaid. *You need to know,* my gut feeling told me, but I didn't want to listen. It would have been too hard to hear the truth. *There I go ignoring my inner voice again.* I was stupid. Even loving Jessie as much as I did— and I loved her to the fullest extent of human love— I didn't take the time to love myself enough not to be involved with her when everyone around me told me not to be.

"What do we do now?" She asked. "Are you willing to work things out?"

I continued my train of thought, not answering her. *What would have happened if I had not followed my heart but my common sense? How different would my life have been? Would I have experienced true love with somebody else?* I felt that our relationship was certainly a natural connection, but it was not a true love. A true love would have been equal from the start. It would have required work and sacrifice to be sure, but nowhere near what I gave up for Jessie. I gave up my dignity. I became a doormat. I gave her my all and only received a fraction of her in return until it was too late. *Pain is what you feel. It hurts. That can't be right.* I remembered the conversation I had with Devonte and the same advice he always had for me over and over: leave Jessie. I had no one to blame for my pain but myself. I stayed because she was familiar. I stayed because I loved her. I stayed because I hoped she would love me back. I…

"Sadira, did you hear me? Are you willing to work things out?"

"I don't know. I have no idea what we do now, but if you're willing to try again, then I am too."

"I really do love you, Sadira. I know that you may not always see or feel it, but I'm telling you right now that I love you more than you will ever know. When you had the car accident, I kept a lot of fear and pain inside because I thought I had to be strong. I was terrified at the thought of losing you. And now with this mess, I guess Kenya was a tool because in her own twisted way she shined a light on us and our flaws. We can't go back to living like robots in the dark, thinking things will fix themselves. I should have shown you how I felt more often."

"I won't wait until I can't take it anymore." I told her.

"It won't ever happen again." She reached for me. "This proves to me that …"

"Proves what?"

She remained silent.

"Proves what?"

"Proves that I need you."

Her words hit me hard but in a good way.   She'd never said that to me. And I could count the number of times she said I love you to me on one hand. I cried. The problem was that I was no longer in love with being love. I would genuinely try to repair our relationship, but I wasn't sure it would work. I needed more. *I need to be alone*, I thought. The idea frightened me. Peace is what I needed, a soft quiet peace that would allow me to take care of myself and would heal me. I knew what was best for me, but I was afriaid to make it happen. Being alone and on my own again was scary.

"Let's just take it one day at a time," I said to her. "It's all we can do."

She nodded and leaned on me. I hugged her, and soon we both fell asleep. It had been a long night.

Fear is such a powerful emotion. Two months went by before anything remotely close to normal resumed between Jessie and me. There was love, as I'm sure there would always be, but we lacked excitement. We barely had any sex, and we'd decided not to talk about Kenya at all. I didn't go to the gym and stopped going to Avery's to make sure I avoided her.

One night Jessie and I went to Bayside to walk by the water and enjoy a warm evening outside. I was waiting for Jessie outside of a restroom when I heard my name.

"Sadira?" It was a female voice.

When I turned, I was face-to-face with Danielle, the intern who had a hand in my losing my job and almost my life.

"Yeah?" I said. She looked nervous and struggled with an apology.

"Don' t worry about it," I said, cutting her off. No, I'm alive and Jessie's here with me." I nodded toward the bathroom.

"You're still with her?"

"Danielle," I said raising my voice.

"Okay, okay. I guess I'll see you around sometime." She turned softly and left before Jessie came out.

"Are you ready?" Jessie asked.

"Yes, I am."

Danielle had disappeared into the mass of people and that was the end of her.

Jessie and I walked hand in hand to my car without speaking. There was a constant voice in my own mind that kept telling me that things would never be the same. Funny, I thought, "the same" had never been fulfilling in the first place. When we got home, we undressed and got ready for bed. We exchanged small talk for a while before she kissed me on the forehead and said goodnight.

Things became a routine with us going to work, paying bills, and planting kisses on the cheek or forehead before going to sleep. We'd become more roommates than lovers though we still shared the same bed.

One day when I came home from work, I saw Jessie packing her personal things in boxes.

"What's going on, Jessie?"

She shook her head slowly, bit her bottom lip, and held back tears.

I really didn't need to ask because I already knew. A part of me sensed that we were heading towards an ending, but I just didn't think it would be this way. Jessie and I were only fooling ourselves thinking that our relationship would return to normal after what happened. Normal was never enough for me anyway. There may be some people who could have survived a situation like ours and live on with a stronger bond, but unfortunately we couldn't. We grew farther apart than I even wanted to admit to myself until our relationship became truly unsalvageable.

"What are you doing, Jessie?" I asked with my voice breaking. I swallowed hard. Tears filled my eyes. "Jessie…"

She sighed, as if she didn't even have enough energy to tell me what I already knew. She just turned to me and touched me gently on my cheek. "Sadira, what happened to us?" I could hear the pain in her voice.

I didn't have an answer to her question, so I remained silent.

She sniffed and wiped her eyes with tissue. "What happened?" Jessie asked again, looking at me earnestly and shaking her head sadly. The mysterious beauty in her blue-gray eyes that I fell in love with looked weighed down with sorrow.

"I don't know," I said. There was no answer and there was nothing I could say that would comfort or sustain either one of us at that moment. I wanted to be able to handle the moment, but I couldn't. I wanted terribly to grab her with all my might and plead with her to stay. I started to cry. My mind told me that ending was right, but my heart remained silent. I was hurting badly on the inside. My heart no longer belonged to Jessie. I didn't know who it belonged to at that point. Maybe it finally belonged to me. I wasn't sure. All I knew was that it no longer told me yes when every other part of me said no. That was it.

"We used to have so much fun," she said. "At least I thought we did, but if you were unhappy for most of the time, then I was sadly wrong."

"I wasn't unhappy most of the time, but…" I didn't finish because I didn't even know what I was going to say. Instead of rambling on, I pulled her down to the couch, and we sat in silence. She put one leg over mine, and I rested my chin on her shoulder.

"What are we going to do?" she asked me.

"Whatever's best," I said to my own surprise. She turned and looked at me. "Whatever's best," I said again to her softly and cried. There was a feeling of downward pressure from which I could not free myself. Depression. I'd never felt it so strongly.

We agreed to sell our home, and Jessie moved out first. She only came around to help show and sell the house. The day she left it felt like my heart was being pulled out of me. The first night without her was torture. Through everything that went on we'd never slept in separate beds, and now I was all alone in the room and bed we shared. I kept reaching and touching the empty space where she used to be. I was delusional, thinking I heard her footsteps in the hall. But no, Jessie was gone, and I was alone with only walls and my moving boxes.

I finally made up my mind to give my job two weeks notice, after we closed on the sale of house. I knew I didn't want to stay in Miami, but I wasn't sure if I wanted to go back to New York either. I decided to move to Atlanta with Khedara. I wanted a fresh start, and Khedara was the only other person I could truly count on. In Atlanta as the days turned into weeks and the weeks turned into a new season, I felt the holidays approach and I always felt emptiness around that time. But these holidays were even worse because all they did was remind me of Jessie. It reminded me of how she changed my life forever and now she was gone. After all dealings with the house were closed we cut off contact with each other.

What do I know about love? I wonder. *Hmm,* I know that I loved Jessie from the moment I laid eyes on her. I had a natural love for Jessie. She didn't have to do anything but exist for me to love her. My attraction and feelings were present without effort or action. It was obvious. It was mysterious. It was present and clear. There was something simply arresting about her presence. Her eyes and smile were extraordinarily beautiful. The way my soul seemed to be constantly sucked into hers still perplexes me. It damaged me to see the look on her face that night she saw Kenya and me together. It was a vision of life ebbing away, leaving her in a desert thirsting for the love she had always been able to count on from me. Those beautiful blue-gray eyes that I'd fallen in love with looked empty and lifeless by the time we ended.

Still, even through the disappointments, I felt deep down there was a reason for us to be together. Was I right or was I wrong? Was I someone in Jessie's life to teach her how to open up? That may very well be the truth, and if it is, then I was *right*. I'll never know. As I sit and think back, I tell myself that Jessie may be the perfect woman, but for someone else. But why did I have to be the woman to prepare her for someone else? Why couldn't I have been "the one" for her? I loved her so much.

Faded images of her presence are etched in my mind as though I were a carbon copy of what we once had, memories filed away for future reference. To this day I feel her. It's like we are attached, and she is everywhere I am. Sometimes I hear her voice inside my head. Laugher, confusion, hurt, exaltation, love, pain, intimacy, and chaos—I know Jessie from every angle, from the surface to the depths. No one understands her the way I did, not even she herself.

A part of me died with our separation. Heartbreak is a kind of death, and I assume that I will be born again, stronger and with inherent knowledge of what is right and wrong in a relationship. Our hearts fought a tumultuous battle with each other. Just wanting to know that Jessie felt the way I did pushed me deeper and deeper into a struggle with myself. So many warnings from my inner voice were ignored. *How could advice from inside of me not be able to penetrate me?* When it came to her, I couldn't even do what I told myself to do. *Through it all though, she was my favorite girl. Strange.*

Perhaps I'll never know if I did the right thing by committing to Jessie. How much different would *her* life had been if I didn't? Maybe she would have never experienced love. *Everyone should experience it at least once.* I felt cheated, though. After all the work I did to make our relationship work, look how it ended. It was unfair. Just thinking about it now makes me want to break down and cry. Sometimes I just want to hide and die alone, but I know that I can't. That would be taking the easy way out.

It is time for me to love myself the way I loved Jessie. I want love again, but I feel so weighted down and afraid to even try again. Where do I begin?

End

I would love to know your thoughts of this book. In fact I am encouraging you to e-mail your comments to: cherilnc@cherilnclarke.com or if you would prefer to write send them to:

Dodi Press – Chaos Comments
244 Fifth Ave., 2nd Floor
Suite J260
New York, NY 10001

Look out for the sequel to *Intimate Chaos*, *Tainted Destiny*! Join the mailing list at www.cherilnclarke.com to be updated with all of my future projects!